5.00

VARIATIONS IN THE NIGHT

Focusing on novels with contemporary concerns, Bantam New Fiction introduces some of the most exciting voices at work today. Look for these titles wherever Bantam New Fiction is sold:

WHITE PALACE by Glenn Savan
SOMEWHERE OFF THE COAST OF MAINE by Ann Hood
COYOTE by Lynn Vannucci
VARIATIONS IN THE NIGHT by Emily Listfield
LIFE DURING WARTIME by Lucius Shepard
(on sale in September)
THE HALLOWEEN BALL by James Howard Kunstler
(on sale in October)

BANTAM NEW FICTION

VARIATIONS IN THE NIGHT

EMILY LISTFIELD

BANTAM BOOKS
TORONTO • NEW YORK • LONDON • SYDNEY • AUCKLAND

VARIATIONS IN THE NIGHT
A Bantam Book / September 1987

Grateful acknowledgment is made for permission to reprint portions of the lyric from "Let's Do It" by Cole Porter, © 1928 Warner Bros. Inc. (Renewed) All Rights Reserved. Used By Permission.

Library of Congress Cataloging-in-Publication Data

Listfield, Emily.
Variations in the night.

(Bantam new fiction)
I. Title.
PS3562.I7822V37 1987 813'.54 87-941
ISBN 0-553-34442-0

Published simultaneously in the United States and Canada

Bantam Books are published by Bantam Books, Inc. Its trademark, consisting of the words "Bantam Books" and the portrayal of a rooster, is Registered in U.S. Patent and Trademark Office and in other countries. Marca Registrada. Bantam Books, Inc., 666 Fifth Avenue, New York, New York 10103.

PRINTED IN THE UNITED STATES OF AMERICA

FG 0 9 8 7 6 5 4 3 2 1

The premature lines cut deep into Sam's cheeks, sharp and clean. Amanda sat back and watched him as he squeezed the lemon peel into his double espresso. "I love this stuff," he said, shaking his head slightly and smiling with a special sense of wonderment and awe—a boy from a flat town in Ohio where the churches gave frequent bridal showers and there were no espresso bars. Sam had been in New York for over a year and it was still a million Christmas mornings to him. He took a sip and looked up at Amanda and bit his lip to keep the same smile from forming. For weeks, he had been dancing gingerly about her, unable to ask her out. He found himself faltering in a way that he was not used to, opening his mouth to suggest a date and emitting a soft string of vowels instead of a time and place. It was as if he needed a new language with her, and he had not yet discovered it. Finally, she had turned to him, amused, impatient. "So look, do you want to go have a cup of coffee?" she had asked.

Now, piercing the usual confines of first-date wariness was this wonderment of Sam's, this enthusiasm. The stained-glass windows of the café were beginning to dull and the little colored lights that draped the room went on and it was strange and romantic and European to him, stranger still because it was a corner stolen from a devastated block and there were hungry people outside. "What a great place," he said as the last notes of a Vivaldi oboe concerto melded into reggae. "Do you come here a lot?"

Amanda tilted her head down so that he could barely see her full lips, curling at the corners. She had cool gray eyes and a steady gaze that seemed to be measuring out what would be given, what would be accepted, marking time. It looked an awful lot like confidence.

"Dumb question," Sam said, more to himself than to her.

For a couple of minutes, they each played with their espressos, dripping it about with tiny baby spoons and wondering what to say.

"So what did you do in Allensville, Ohio?" Amanda asked finally as she uncrossed her legs and lit a cigarette.

"I was a reporter for the local paper."

"How come you left?"

"I guess I figured there had to be something more important to write about than state fairs."

Sam ordered another espresso and began to describe what it was like to work for the Allensville *Weekly Ledger*, what it was like to stay home. He spoke slowly in low tones that suggested an intimacy that did not of course exist and Amanda found herself leaning forward on the wobbly marble table, holding her head and her cigarette in the same hand, listening intently. There was a softness in his voice that held her more than what he was saying and the willingness in it tugged at her like nostalgia. He had straight blond hair and shiny marble eyes and he made her laugh about the ancient Allensville society columnist who started every paragraph with a quote from Shakespeare and sometimes ended with one too.

"And I thought there was no civilization in the Midwest," Amanda said.

"Well, the column only appears once every two years. That more than covers Allensville's society." Sam leaned forward. "And what do you want to be when you grow up?"

"Younger than I am now."

"No, really."

Amanda lit another cigarette. She had rummaged about for a goal for years and the only one she had ever been able to come up with was this: to be self-contained. Anything more than that eluded her and now she was almost thirty and she figured she was too old to play with those particular building blocks.

"What makes you think I want to be anything? My job's not so bad." She was working at the moment at Legacies, a small clothing store owned by a mutual friend.

"You just don't look like the type to be all that interested in fashion." Perhaps he had read her all wrong. He certainly hadn't meant to insult her.

Amanda looked at him and looked at what she was wearing and she laughed. Her sweater, her coat, most of her clothes, in fact, were unraveling. They were not bad clothes, they had once been good clothes, but now they were all unraveling. She knew too that she could pull it off, that she could rim her eyes with liner and shuffle about her feathery light brown hair and it would be okay.

"I guess I'm not. I'm just helping Nancy out for a while."

"And then?"

Amanda pushed her cup away and shrugged. Looking up, she shook her head sharply as if to get rid of the conversation and motioned to the waitress for a check. There was nothing for Sam to do but follow. They walked a few blocks together through the gray city dusk filled with the smells of smog and sex that catches you and then vanishes like the sparkling glass fragments in the pavement.

Amanda sat at the bar smoking a cigarette and concentrating very hard on the ashtray. The man next to her had been edging closer since she got her drink and she was in no mood. Reflexively, she had checked him out. Stringy graying hair slicked behind his ears, baggy jeans that were belted too low, a three-day stubble—a leftover beat, he wouldn't be so bad-looking but for the wash of debauchery.

"Where are you from?" he asked, pulling his beer up intimately next to hers.

"Here."

"You're kidding me."

"Some people are actually from New York."

"Well what are you doing here?" It was unclear whether he meant this bar or this city. It didn't much matter.

"Hanging out."

He laughed. "When were you born?"

"Fifty-eight."

"Well I've been hanging out here since fifty-nine. I've been hanging out since you were a toddler."

"Then you must be an expert at it. A regular Ph.D. of hanging out."

Amanda saw Nancy coming in and waved to her with relief. As her friend settled in, Amanda turned her back on the doctor and laughed. She too was something of an expert at hanging out. In fact, she had begun to think it was the only thing that she had any real talent for. She was in no mood.

"How did it go?"

"What?"

"Your date with Sam. How did it go?"

"He reminds me of Dennis the Menace."

"C'mon, Amanda," Nancy said, laughing despite herself. "Would I have introduced you if he didn't have potential? Give him a chance. Besides, I hear he's pretty talented. He might just be good for you."

Amanda frowned. She often had the feeling of having missed something a long time ago and now it was too late to have it that way, the way it should have been, all fresh and moist, and what she missed was this—being a girl who has a boy. She'd had many lovers, but they had all been the ephemeral addictions of the night with no claims in the morning. At sixteen, she had eagerly given away her virginity to the first bidder—a boy she had met two days before—and there had been no romance that night or the next time with the next boy or the time after that.

And so at some point she came to assume that this was something she was incapable of—being a girl who has a boy—it was something other girls were and she never seemed to be and if she never quite understood it, she came to accept it as one accepts a birthmark. Only lately, lately . . .

"Well?" Nancy asked.

"I told him I'd go out with him this weekend."

"Careful—your enthusiasm might ignite the bar."

"Listen, are you going to buy me a drink or do I have to play footsie with Doctor Feelgood over there?"

Sam sat at the desk he shared with two other free-lancers and went through the mangled stack of invitations trying to find one suitable for the evening. They came in the shapes of Fabergé eggs and film canisters and miniature Corvettes and some were even edible, though the senior staffers usually took those first—one of the job's fringe benefits. It was late Friday afternoon and Sam could tell by the large assortment of fingerprints that all of the really good invitations were gone. He chose a box of crayons that contained the promise of the ultimate playground party and stuck it in his back pocket.

Amanda hadn't finished dressing when he arrived and he sat in the living room while she changed her shoes from red to black to red again. When she finally came back out, he looked appreciatively at her—softly askew in her man's sweater, her hair already coming undone and falling across her pale eyebrows—and she smiled slightly and asked, "So where are we going, anyway?" Sam showed her the box of crayons and noticed that her mouth fell just a little on opening it. "Is something wrong?" he asked. "No," Amanda said as she handed him back the crayons. "It's fine."

Sam realized what was wrong as soon as they got

there. The club was only half filled with businessmen on expense accounts and girls from the suburbs wandering in and out of the many rooms, asking each other, "Did you know this used to be a church?" A few of the waiters were wearing skirts just to be sure there would be something to talk about and one of the bartenders was dressed up as a Barbie doll. It was a club on its way out—you could feel it leaning precipitously, a little bit more each night—and you could feel too the owners' groaning efforts to pull it back up.

Sam and Amanda stood on the sidelines and watched the flickering orange and blue geometric patterns that the lights made on the dancers' backs. Amanda remembered other nights, nights when the club was new and sharp, and she said to Sam, "It didn't used to be this way." But Sam had never been there before and only shrugged his shoulders. "Did you know this used to be a church?" he asked. Amanda suggested that they dance.

They walked out onto the dance floor and slid inside the throbbing rhythm, losing themselves to it as if to a third person. Sam moved confidently, smoothly, his compact torso bucking in perfect time with the beat, just within reach of Amanda's long arms, swaying in mid-air as if supported by water. Every now and then they looked up from their half-closed eyes and caught each other watching, noting, both obviously pleased with what they found, and they smiled with freshly minted approval and moved a little closer.

And yet, when the music changed and a slower song filled the room and other couples fell readily into each other, they both agreed that it was time to leave.

The cool night air clung to their damp hair and faces, making them both feel glossy and alert. They walked slowly back to Amanda's apartment without talking about it, as if they did not notice where they were going.

Inside, Amanda poured them both a drink and sat down at the dining-room table and Sam, who had been heading for the couch, followed suit.

"I like the magazine you work for," Amanda said. She had begun to doodle nervously with a fountain pen.

"It's okay," Sam said, a little bit disdainfully. He still had his coat on and he jingled the change about in his pockets. "I'd much rather be doing something else."

"What?"

"I'd really like to cover city politics," Sam said. "That's what I set out to do."

Amanda laughed. "Well, the VIP rooms of clubs seem like a good place to start."

"I'm serious." Sam was frowning now.

"Sorry." Amanda looked up from the endless scrawls forming before her and watched Sam for a minute, intrigued, wondering what it was like to want something the way he wanted something.

She watched too the way his eyes followed her when she moved, when she lifted her hair off of her neck or reached for her wine or crossed her legs, his eyes followed, looking for openings. He must want her—he watched so closely, looking for lesions, looking for clues—and yet he sat with his coat still on and he did not move toward her.

"It's late," he said finally. "I'd better get going."

And as they stood by the open door, she moved hastily to kiss him good night, and just as hastily, she withdrew, just as his lips began looking for openings, looking for clues.

At thirteen, Amanda had still been thin and hard and flat. Sally, a year younger, had already begun to swell and she would strut around her older sister, sticking out her new curves. She was all external motion, laughing and light and playing by any rule she could find. For unlike Amanda, Sally found the rituals of security the most powerful seduction of all and she set about to find them, to revere and uphold them, for inside security there must be security.

Amanda had reluctantly agreed to go out with Sally and Frank. They had gotten a babysitter for their eighteen-month-old daughter, Maggie, and Frank played a video trivia game while the two sisters talked.

"You look good," Sally said. "I like your hairdo."

Amanda self-consciously removed the plastic pearl barrette that held up the left side of her hair in a halo of loose ends. "Thanks."

"So tell me," Sally said, resting her elbows on the sticky maroon table. "How's your love life?"

"The same."

"The same," Sally said, mimicking her sister and dropping her shoulders in despair. "The same as what? Mata Hari?"

"Jesus, Sally." Amanda stuck her forefinger in her drink and stirred it around.

"I'm sorry. But you know what I mean."

"Well if you must know, I did meet someone new," Amanda said, surprising herself as much as Sally.

"That's great." Sally's voice was softer now, encouraging. "What's he like?"

Just as Amanda was about to think up an answer, Frank came back and slid in next to his wife. "How'd you do, honey?" Sally asked, slipping her arm through his.

"I won," Frank answered stiffly.

"That's wonderful." Sally kissed him on the cheek.

Amanda ordered another drink and held her tongue as they set about discussing disposable nipples, dhurrie rugs, nursery school applications, single neighbors who played their music too loud, until it was finally time to go home.

Alone, she drank brandy from a mug in bed, glad of the darkness, the silence. But she woke at four A.M., scared and edgy. Scared of burglars and cancer and the cats crying outside her window and wrinkles. Scared of her own lonesomeness. She turned on the radio and closed her eyes, drifting off while strangers raged about their sex lives, the mayor, MX missiles . . .

In the morning, she pierced a capsule of vitamin E and spread the grease beneath her eyes. But all this seemed to do was make the dark circles glisten.

A certain reserve, a certain caution, continued to snake through Amanda and Sam's beginning. They parried with each other and they parried with time and they both felt somewhat out of step, clumsy.

When Sam didn't call her for five days, Amanda found herself going over and over their last date, wondering what she had said or done wrong. She was used to men desiring her, courting her, clinging to her, trying to capture her. But she was not used to Sam's timing, the slow carefulness that governed his words and precluded any caresses. "For Christ's sake," Nancy said finally. "Why don't you just call him?" Amanda gave a little laugh. "I'm not that kind of girl," she said, and Nancy rolled her eyes.

Sam finally called two nights later. "I'm sorry I haven't called all week," he said. "I've been really busy."

"Yeah, me too," Amanda said immediately.

"Would you like to have dinner tomorrow night?"

"Sure."

They sat beneath the drooping fronds of a fake palm tree drinking rum punches in the stuffed Caribbean restaurant, talking more animatedly than they had before.

"It was a gas," Sam said. He had been telling Amanda

about going up in a little Cessna two-seater with an old barnstormer he had once been sent to interview. "She even let me do some of the flying."

"Weren't you scared?"

"There was dual control. Besides, I was having too much fun to think about it. I'd really love to learn how to fly one day."

"Are you serious?"

Sam smiled. "I know you have me written off as just another greenhorn, but . . ."

Amanda bit the straw that had been dangling from her lips and smiled guiltily down into the pink slush of her drink.

Their dinner came and they moved on to other topics as they ate—foreign policy and French movie stars and the people waiting at the door—but through it all, Amanda was waiting anxiously for one moment, the moment that obliterates all other words and plans and intentions, when two people know they will make love. At least she would know the rules then. She was patient at first, then she tried to manufacture it, leaning across the table with a look, a touch, an unbuttoned button, and then she went back to waiting. But if Sam was aware of these efforts, he did not let on. He wanted to push the moment back, just a little bit back, and so in his hands there was coldness. The moment arrived, though, despite their sooner/later efforts.

Sam reached over and gently fingered the bangs away from Amanda's eyes. "Let's go back to dry land," he said. He put his arm around Amanda and steered her protectively out from under the palm tree's shade just as another couple pounced greedily on their empty chairs.

Sam had sublet a loft in Tribeca from an actor he knew from Allensville and now he took Amanda there for the first time. There was a sense of romance to it, with its big country kitchen and its wall of windows, with its soft bed in the middle blocked off by flowering plants. Dark rugs and couches gave it a sense of quiet and stability that neither cared to question.

They made love slowly. Tentatively. Lights from the bar across the street filtered through the venetian blinds and remade smudgy lines across their bodies. Looking down at Sam's head between her breasts, Amanda thought it was so sweet it was like the movies. But just as they had parried with words and with time and not found their rhythm, that was what the night was like too. They were both solicitous and kind and vaguely disappointed.

Unlike Amanda, Sam had had few lovers. Maybe three or four.

"Once," he said, "once I went a year and a half without sex."

"How come?"

"I wasn't in love with anyone. I tried a couple of times, but I couldn't do it. Literally."

"I haven't heard that one before," Amanda said dryly, and yet she was oddly touched by his confession.

In the morning, Sam made small forays into affection, but when he kissed her shoulder he could feel the muscles tighten and he withdrew. Amanda had become used to a world where only the act was important and it was usually an act of defiance. She could not quite believe the sincerity of the kiss and it confused her and it also made her quiver deep inside, deeper than she had all night, and she wanted to leave right away. "I'm late," she said, pulling her clothes on carelessly. "I'd better run." And she slid sideways through the door.

Sam was left alone with the breakfast he had planned for two, perplexed by the way she seemed to hand out warmth in only the cleanest, most carefully measured doses, and then leave—with no imprint of the night. He made up the bed and went to work.

He called her that evening because that is what men are supposed to do, call a woman after spending the night with her, and also because he wanted to talk to her. Nancy answered the phone. "It's Sam," she yelled in to Amanda, who was busy rubbing her eyes to see if her new smudgeproof blue mascara would smudge. "What does he want?" Amanda asked with mock disdain.

"How should I know? To talk over old times?"

Amanda came to the phone with flakes of navy blue circling her eyes and falling onto her cheeks.

"Hi. I just called to, you know, say hello. See how your day was." Sam's voice was soft and nervous.

"Fine. Busy. You know." Amanda was nervous too and terse.

"I had a good time last night."

"Me too."

"Would you like to go to the movies later?"

"Thanks, but I already made other plans."

"Oh. Well. How about Friday or Saturday?"

"Sure. Give me a call."

"Okay. Good night."

"Good night."

Amanda hung up and turned to Nancy. "You doing anything tonight?"

"Not that I know of."

"Good. Let's go check out that new club uptown."

Which they did. But despite her best efforts to drown it out, the faltering disappointment in Sam's voice lingered into the evening.

Sam drank his beer slowly. The fabled newspaper bar that he had been dying to see was dark and sour-smelling and Amanda was late. He looked hopefully at the door each time it swung open, and each time, the red-faced man next to him turned his head too.

"I'm waiting for someone," Sam said.

"Who isn't?"

"No. I mean someone specific."

The man shrugged. "Suit yourself," he said and ordered another J.D. on the rocks.

Finally, Amanda arrived. Sam watched the outline of her long legs pushing against a slim skirt as she took quick and certain strides toward him. She started talking before he had a chance to kiss her hello.

"I'm sorry I'm so late," she said. "I ran into this guy I haven't seen in ages and he had a bloody nose and I had to take him . . . Well, you know how it is." She was finally sitting down now.

Sam didn't quite know how it was but he smiled politely and said it was okay.

"So this is it," Amanda said as she looked around the near-empty bar. "I've always been curious about this place."

Sam was suddenly embarrassed for wanting to come

here, embarrassed for not knowing better. "Maybe it wasn't such a great idea after all."

"What's the matter, doesn't it make you feel inspired?"

He looked over to see if she was making fun of him for he was never quite sure if she was or not but she was smiling and it wasn't a mean smile. It was a half-smile that puzzled him and also made him want to kiss her, but she didn't make it easy. "Why don't we go someplace else?" he said.

"Are you sure? I'd be happy to stay here." She hadn't meant to cut him. In fact, she had liked it that he had wanted to come here, that he had places to go that meant something more than a mention in a gossip column. But it wasn't something she could say.

"No," Sam said as he put some bills down on the bar. "But it's lady's choice next."

They walked a few blocks uptown and Amanda would not tell him where they were going. "Someplace I used to go when I was a kid" was all she would say. "Someplace I haven't been to in years." It seemed that kind of day.

"Jesus," Sam said as they got off the elevator on the 65th floor and entered the Rainbow Room. They sat at a small table by the window and took turns standing up and peering over the railing at the black and white candy town beneath them.

"You didn't really come here when you were a kid, did you?"

"Sure," Amanda said, laughing gently. "My father used to bring me. Until he became persona non grata."

"What happened?"

There was that half-smile again, her strange half-smile that was at once mocking and resigned. "A lot of broken glass under the bridge."

"What?"

Amanda looked at Sam, looked at his handsome face chiseled as if made with a very steady hand, now so open and so curious, and she started to lean forward. Once, her father had been a magician, full of dreams and tall tales. He was going to take the family and move to India and they would be draped in silk and waited on by servants. He was going to move them to New Orleans and open up a night club filled with exotic dancers and rich tourists and they would sway to the saxophone in one long summer night. He would bring them to a shingled beach house and he would write a best seller and they would be the toast of New York in the newest cocktail dresses . . . "Never mind," Amanda said abruptly and she stood up to look out the window. "It was a long time ago." She didn't know why she had brought him here to begin with.

Sam stayed seated, watching her profile reflected in the glass, the straight lines of her nose and her square chin softened and blurry. In a minute, she turned around with her hands on her hips. "Any other big-city sights you'd like to see tonight, sir?"

"I can think of one or two."

Their senses were numbed by the afternoon's liquor and all about them now were other couples, crisp, matching, easy couples. Amanda and Sam fell against each other in the elevator, leanness on leanness, laughing and kissing lightly as their ears popped.

At Amanda's apartment, they made their way on jelly legs down the narrow hallway and into the small bedroom in the back. The only window looked out on an alleyway, but nevertheless, there was a shade and a venetian blind on top of that and everything was drawn tight, as if nailed permanently shut. Sam hit his shinbone on the corner of the bed and swore loudly but he didn't ask her to turn on the lights and she didn't offer to. They collapsed onto the bed and onto each other and they fumbled blindly about, trying to find zippers, buttons, lips, but it was so dark that they seemed somehow to miss each other.

They began to see each other two times a week, some times three times a week, and Amanda was gradually beginning to find pleasure in the very ordinariness of being part of a couple, of the way Sam would take her hand while waiting on line for a movie or put his arm around her while walking down the street and not just alone in the night. Sometimes, he left a book behind in her apartment and then she would place it neatly on the table and it was as if a spotlight caught on this piece of Sam and she would touch it when she passed by. She smiled to herself when she thought of him, always with a paperback sticking out of his pocket, Raymond Chandler this week, Petronius the week before, smiled when she thought of the way he underlined in yellow Magic Marker like a college kid and tried to make her sit still while he read aloud from his latest obsession. "Listen to this," he would say as he paced excitedly up and down the room, "you've got to listen to this . . ." And she would nod and try to listen but she was really watching the way his lips moved.

But still, she could not admit to this enthusiasm, it would be too dangerous. And so in her efforts to hide and to master it, she put a limit on her movements, her actions. She was unable to initiate affection, to take his hand first, to speak first of "us." She watched herself carefully and she watched him and they found themselves embarked on a program of emotional austerity.

It was as if they were touching hands on either side of a prison wall. Though each determined that this time, this evening, they would break through, feel skin on skin, when they got together something stiffened and they were a marionette couple. Only sometimes, in the night, did the awkwardness disappear and so both came to long for the anonymity of darkness, for the freedom it could bring. But more often than not, they were unable to melt into each other and they had clumsy marionette sex too.

Sam was not Amanda's only lover. There were Bill and Peter too, and she was slow to relinquish them. Neither had the slightest expectation of her, nor she of them, and so there was a certain abandon that was missing with Sam. When they asked her what she liked, they only meant this very second and that was all the responsibility there was. When she made love with Bill, or with Peter, it was not about trials or questions or hopes or insinuations. It was simply what it was—fucking in the night.

Amanda lay half off the bed, smoking a cigarette. It was one A.M. and she thought Sam was asleep.

"Are you sleeping with anyone else?" he asked.

She flicked her ashes and kept her back to him. "No."

They had not spoken about fidelity, but it was something that Sam naturally took for granted. Though now he was not so sure.

"Just tell me the truth."

"Does it matter to you?"

"I don't know. Tell me and then I'll know."

She turned to him. "What about you? Are you sleeping with anyone else?"

"No." Silence. "So who is it?"

"What difference does it make? Just some guys."

"Some guys? Plural?"

She lit another cigarette. "There's safety in numbers," she muttered.

He ignored this. "Who are they? Do they have names?"

"No. They don't have names. Look, I don't know why you're making such a big deal about this. It's not like we made any promises to each other. Right?"

"Right. Please excuse me. My mistake. But as long as we're on the subject, do you plan on continuing? With them, I mean."

"I don't know. It's not very important. No. Okay?"

"Okay."

What she had wanted to say was this: There are so many kinds of sex and we don't seem to be having any of them. There is hard and new like there is no tomorrow and there is slow and all-night like there are endless tomorrows and there are so many more and why don't we seem to be having any of them?

And he would have said the same thing. For the woman he had first been attracted to, the woman with the steady gaze and the amused look and the confident walk was not the one he found and wherever she was, she was always too far away and he could never seem to reach her.

But neither of them said anything more that night.

In the morning, they sat together on the couch, drinking their coffee in an uneasy silence. When Amanda got up to get them refills, Sam stood up too and walked over to the phone. "I think I'll check in with my service," he said. "What's my number again?"

"225-8090," Amanda answered automatically.

"Ah hah," he said triumphantly.

Amanda looked at Sam and realized that she had been trapped. "Well . . ."

"Don't worry." Sam laughed indulgently. "I've memorized your number too."

Amanda scrunched her bare toes, annoyed and embarrassed. "Since when do you have a service anyway?"

"I don't," Sam said, smiling still. "Do you think I should get one? I kind of like the way it sounds."

Amanda had to laugh.

The color of hot summer afternoons when it is piercing yellow bright outside, almost white, but you don't care because you are lying inside with all of the blinds closed so it is an even grayish tan and the sun is just a rumor.

That is the color Amanda wanted all of her mornings to be. She had never quite conquered the rhythms of daylight, she did not understand its rules of dress and quickness. In the daylight, her pale skin often looked pasty and her eyes dull and it was the only time she moved with any heaviness. If in the night people came to her and it was hers, she had to be careful in the morning not to fall.

There was the faintest of scars on Amanda's right cheek, just below her eye, that she had gotten by falling off of a bicycle twenty years ago and on certain mornings it seemed more pronounced than others, though no one had ever noticed it. This was one of those mornings and she leaned over the sink and smoothed foundation carefully over her face. When she was done with her makeup she went inside and dressed for work in loose black wool pants and a navy shirt and black ankle boots that laced up like Mary Poppins'. Other than the light tooled cowboy belt about her hips, her clothes were dark, soft and draped, and just a little somber. She never seemed to look quite in fashion or out of fashion—the sleeve that was meant to be buttoned down was pushed up, the lipstick was last year's color, or was it next year's—and yet there was a grace that many of the women who came into the store and spent ten times more than she on clothes would gladly have traded for. Nevertheless, they felt at ease with her, for there was not the judgmental disdain of *Vogue*-addicted salesgirls, and if there was any mockery, it did not show. She turned off the radio and left the apartment, only fifteen minutes late.

Legacies was still basically a neighborhood shop and it suited Amanda. She enjoyed talking to the people who wandered in, especially if they had no interest in buying anything, and she was relieved too by the fact that she had little real responsibility. Of course, Nancy had other plans for her, but she could be put off for a while. In the meantime, she didn't have to take it too seriously and it was just enough so that she didn't have to think about doing something else. Luckily, her family had money, the invisible kind of money that you never quite see but know is there, the kind that makes it seem automatic to skip from job to job. If you're not happy, why not?

After work, she took a cab up to 73rd Street and got out in front of a large old apartment building. Upstairs, she opened the door with her own key. Her mother's apartment was dimly lit and it smelled like the inside of a suitcase that had not been opened for a very long time.

Amanda and her mother sat in the living room with a cracking cardboard hatbox filled with old photographs. Her mother picked up one picture after another, lifting her glasses and bringing it close to her eyes.

Here she is, the sweater girl, with this boy and with this one.

"Who's he?" Amanda asked. She had never really thought of her mother with anyone but her father.

"I don't remember. I was in the U.S.O. Everyone was."

And she held up another—here she is at a milk bar with her waved hair so pretty and the soldier boy so young and so blond.

"What do you see?" she asked her daughter.

"Innocence."

"Exactly."

Mrs. Easton put the photographs back in the box. She was a thin, breakable woman with graying hair and proper skirts and Amanda was shocked at how robust she had once been.

"And what of your young man? Your sister tells me you're seeing someone new."

Amanda laughed. She had always kept her young men separate. She had compartmentalized her life—day, night, family, lovers—she had rarely let them overlap.

"He's not my young man."

"You mean you're not seeing him anymore?"

"I mean people don't belong to each other."

"Of course they do."

"The way you and Dad belonged to each other?"

Mrs. Easton stood up. She did not wish to discuss the divorce, any more than she would discuss her husband's alcoholism. It was not the done thing. She had gambled on a handsome, vague young man—and lost. It was a personal defeat, not the fault of Marriage, that it had turned into twenty years of the small failures and stony recriminations that had led her here—righteous and alone.

She looked over at her daughter, so certain and unyielding. Even as a child, she had made sure nothing would stick to her. There was Amanda, fulfilling obligations and walking between the breaches and leaving as soon as possible.

"When did you strike loneliness from the bargain?" Mrs. Easton asked.

Sam came from no money, no money at all. He had been taught early and repeatedly that the constants in life were duty, obligation, debt. He had gone to the local university, which was expected, and majored in English, which was tolerated. His mother's one true disappointment was that her only son had stopped growing at 5′10″. "He'll go out for baseball instead," Mr. Chapman said, trying to console his wife. "It's just not the same, Fred." Mrs. Chapman lived for basketball.

At twenty-eight, Sam had found himself comfortably ensconced as one of the more talented reporters at the Allensville *Weekly Ledger,* finally free of various loans and debts for the first time in his adult life and talking about marriage with his girl. Everything was falling neatly into place, everything was as it should be.

One Sunday afternoon, he was sitting on the porch with his grandmother, eating pecans and listening to her gossip about the weekly historical society meeting's never-ending battle to preserve Allensville's character. "I do wish you'd take an interest," she had said. "It's never too early to start." Suddenly he saw that this was it, this porch, these pecans, this would always be it. Within the next month, he had abruptly given notice to the paper, the girl, and his confused family. It was the first really foolhardy thing he had ever done.

He had been in New York for fourteen months now and the only steady work he had been able to find was writing for *Backlog,* one of the newer, consciously offbeat fashion/gossip journals, the type that used the model's first name and made you feel that you had just had dinner with her and it was the most amusing dinner ever, and by the way, don't you want the dress? Sam had no personal interest in fashion whatsoever; he himself had few clothes, though they were always neat and well pressed, and this certainly wasn't what he had hoped to be doing. And yet he'd been glad of the job at first, not just because of the money or the connections he hoped it would bring, but because he was fascinated by this new kind of model, this new girl who would be considered an oddity at best back in Ohio, this girl who felt no seeming obligation to beauty but whose illicit haughtiness made the conventions of beauty irrelevant. She fascinated him, with her strange clothes and her stranger hairdos, the way the sight of a prostitute had fascinated him when he was twelve.

It was eight o'clock at night when Sam finished the assignment due the next day and since he had the keys to the West Village offices, he figured he might as well walk over and leave the italicized sentences and exclamation points on the editor's desk. At the last minute, he decided to call Amanda. "Do you want to come?" he asked. "Sure," she said eagerly. "It's Nancy's favorite magazine."

The offices were dark and cluttered and Sam and Amanda tiptoed about, whispering and giggling like mischievous children. Sam was ready to leave when Amanda caught sight of the clothes, irresponsibly left out after a shoot, the clothes with their nursery school colors and their harsh geometric shapes like the Jetsons, cut up into fringes and mini-skirts, reminiscent, Sam was sure, of the sixties, though certainly not of any sixties he had been through. Without asking him, Amanda started to unzip her jeans, unbutton her blouse, until she was standing in the partially lit neon office in only her cowboy boots and underwear. She chose first a black skirt of buttery leather and, skipping over the shirts, put on a purple fringed cowboy jacket with a $1,200 price tag dangling from the zipper. She spit into her hands and rubbed her hair back as far as it would go and then she went looking for a mirror.

Sam was mesmerized into silence, watching the self-absorption, and watching too Amanda in the first convincingly spontaneous act he had ever caught her in. When she noticed his eyes in the mirror, though, carefully observing her, she turned away self-consciously. "I'd better change back." Sam walked toward her. "Wait a minute. I think I know where they keep the liquor." After trying a few drawers unsuccessfully, he found a good bottle of scotch and they sat on the floor and drank it out of plastic cups.

"All you need now is a mechanical bull," he said.

"You'll do." She reached over suddenly and kissed him firmly on the lips. "You'll do just fine," she whispered and kissed him again and it was the first time he was sure, really sure, that she wanted him. He held her away for a moment, as if to verify, but what he saw was not quite her, not quite Amanda, but a starkly modern urban cowgirl.

He pulled her quickly back to him so that he would not have to think too much about it and they made love on the cool and dusty linoleum floor.

Afterward, he found the bottle of scotch in a bed of purple fringes, took a swig, and wiped his mouth with the back of his hand. "Boy," he said. Amanda laughed and reached over to straighten his tousled hair. "A rough night at the office, dear?" she said as she pressed her forehead to his.

Amanda and Nancy were unpacking and sorting a new group of patterned rayon shirts that had just come in. It was early afternoon and over the store's tape deck, Ella Fitzgerald was scatting in and around Cole Porter. "People say in Boston even beans do it . . ."

"I sneezed," Nancy said disgustedly.

"So?"

"So I could just feel all those millions of sperm shooting out of me."

"Oh c'mon."

"Okay. So it's not millions. It's thousands. But all I want is one. Is that too much for a girl to ask for?"

"It'll happen," Amanda said reassuringly.

"Yeah, well, we're both getting pretty sick of trying. Do you want to come over for dinner tonight? Jack would love to see you. In fact, Jack would love to see anyone who doesn't ramble on about temperature charts."

Amanda laughed. "Thanks. You sure know how to make me feel wanted."

"Sorry, bad mood. My husband and I would appreciate the pleasure of your company at dinner this evening."

"It would be my honor."

"Good. Look, will you go take care of that customer

by the door? I want to go back and straighten out these order forms."

Amanda always experienced a split second of surprise, the slightest of shocks, when Nancy referred to Jack as "my husband." They had been married for over three years, so it could no longer be the newness of it, but still, she just didn't think of them that way—the Martins—that's not how she thought of them, of Nancy, at all. Nancy was still her singular partner, the one she called when she had a new pair of patent leather shoes that were begging to go dancing all night. And it was still Nancy who went.

When Amanda arrived at Nancy and Jack's loft, she found them both sitting on the floor of Jack's study, glueing sequins onto the naked felt shells of hats. Minuscule flecks of black and fuchsia glimmered from their fingertips, their knees, their hair, even the leaves of a nearby plant. "Frustration," Nancy moaned, acknowledging the glittery begonia. "Dinner's going to be a little late. I'd really like to get some more of these done." Jack poured Amanda a glass of wine and she picked up a tube of glue and a hat.

Often when it was the three of them like this, Amanda felt vaguely apologetic for her presence, and so she was glad for this common task. She liked Jack, with his sardonic humor and his lawyer's analytical nature, and she knew that he liked her, but often she found herself talking just a little bit louder than normal, trying just a little bit harder to keep his interest, make him laugh, as if to make up for the missing fourth, the missing male. And there were times too when she didn't know quite where to look. When Nancy kissed the top of his head, when Jack took a particularly heavy plate from Nancy's hands, when they used their own personal shorthand to discuss the specifics of their day—it was these little acts of protection that husband and wife committed without even noticing it, these natural touches and sentences with which they took care of each other, that made Amanda visibly uncomfortable. And when, at the end of a particularly rough day, Nancy said, "I really need Jack to hold me," Amanda bristled slightly. It was alien, this certainty of the other. She could not even imagine it.

Their hands were white and caked and sticky now. Shimmering cloches hung at precarious angles from Jack's law books and desk corners, proud and wet. Nancy picked up her glass of wine and saw that there were tiny hot pink islands floating in the Chardonnay. "Ah, the glamorous life," she said. The three of them washed their hands together in the kitchen sink and finally sat down to a good, if somewhat haphazard dinner.

Later, as Amanda stood at the door waiting for the freight elevator to come and take her down, Jack said, "Why don't you bring Sam next time?"

Amanda cringed in exaggerated horror. "What? Introduce him to the family? I wouldn't want him to get any funny ideas."

"Seriously," Jack pushed on. "At least Nancy knows him. But I hardly ever get to meet your boyfriends. Are you ashamed of me?"

"Terribly. No, actually I'm just protecting you. Half of them have contagious diseases."

"Well you've been seeing this one for almost two months now. For you that constitutes a serious involvement. I think it's time I check him out."

Amanda laughed. But this little inkling of protectiveness had made her warm and shy and pleased as a young coquette. "Maybe next time," she said.

When she got off the phone with her father, Amanda went out and bought two packs of cigarettes and tried to have her Valium prescription refilled despite the fact that the bottle clearly said "No refills." Then she had coffee at the local diner, scanning the want ads, the personal ads, the apartment ads, while she drank and smoked. She wasn't looking for anything in particular, not really. She just liked knowing that there was something else out there. It was one of the things she did.

Back home, she sat by the phone and lit yet another cigarette, though her throat was already sandpapered red and sore. Slowly, she dialed Sally's number.

"Maggie's just about to get up from her nap," Sally said breathlessly. She always sounded breathless and Amanda wondered what it was that kept her so busy. "Can you make it quick?"

"Dad called me this morning."

"Oh?" Sally's voice was lower now and she was sitting down. "Where has he been?"

"Connecticut."

"Connecticut?"

"He bought a little house there."

"I hardly see him as the country squire." Sally's anger

was poking through and through, bouncing like rubber bullets off Amanda's determinedly calm and even voice.

"Look, Sally," Amanda said. "He's getting married."

"He's what? Jesus, I didn't even think the divorce was final yet. That bastard. How can he do that to Mom?"

"You know that they decided on the divorce together."

Sally did not care to get into all that again. "Does he plan on telling me this?" she asked.

"I think he's scared to. He asked me to do it."

"I see. Well who is she?"

"Someone he met at A.A."

"Oh great, he's back to that, is he? Well he's been to A.A. before, you know. All he ever did was come home and make fun of the way people said, 'Hi, Bob.' "

"Sally, will you please calm down? The least you can do is hope that he stays sober. I think he really means it this time."

"Right. What about Mom?"

"He wants us to tell her."

"I don't believe it. What an unbelievable coward."

"I think we should go over there tonight. Okay?"

In the background, Amanda could hear Maggie bawling and Sally was breathless again. "What time?"

"How about six? And Sally, can you please try to keep the histrionics to a minimum?"

Sally hung up without answering.

Two hours later, Mrs. Easton stood with her back to her daughters, twisting and twisting her slim gold wedding band. She hadn't yet been able to take it off. Tomorrow, she would promise herself, I'll take it off tomorrow. Now she eased it up over her knuckle and then pushed it home again and then eased it back up. She did not ask questions—what does she look like, how long have they known each other, who is she, who is she?—she just twisted and pulled her ring in silence. Finally, in a barely audible voice, she said, "What?" She looked at Amanda and then at Sally in childlike incomprehension. "What?"

"He's marrying someone else," Sally said loudly, and impatient for a reaction, any reaction, she started to cry herself.

"Oh. Oh well yes. I suppose that is just what he should do." Mrs. Easton turned full face now and smiled. "How is my granddaughter?" she asked.

The two sisters left soon afterward. They listened to the wheezes and groans of the aging building as they waited for the elevator and they did not look each other in the eye. Only when they were out on the street did they begin to speak.

"Do you want to go someplace and have a drink?" Amanda asked.

"No," Sally said. "I have to go home and fix dinner for my husband."

It was obvious that she had already had a couple of drinks before she called him. Actually, it was only after the second that the possibility had even occurred to her—she was so unused to having someone to turn to. "Let's go hear some music," she said. But it was flat and imperative and it was far from casual. In fact, it was the closest thing to "Please hold my hand. I need you" that Sam had heard.

Amanda was walking a few steps ahead of him now, walking fast and hard and defiantly, as if she might break into a run at any moment. Sam hung back and watched her boot heels gnash at the pavement. It was only when she was forced to stop for a red light that they were really next to each other and he took hold of her arm. "Did something happen today?" he asked.

She looked at him quizzically, having no idea how to stop what was spiraling inside and give it to him. "No."

"You sure?"

"I don't want to talk about it." She was impatient for the light to change. She wanted only to be moving, moving fast.

"Amanda?"

"It's not that big a deal. My father's getting remarried

and I had to tell my mother."

"How did she take it?"

"She didn't."

Amanda led Sam to a club that they had never been to before. They walked down some uneven steps strewn with graffiti and broken beer bottles and pried open a thick metal door. Sam thought of Harlem, of speakeasies, of secret names and vices. "Do we have to say Joe sent us?" he asked.

Darkness and smoke and music hit them full face, like a wave, knocking their breath out, making them unsure of their feet for a moment. The music was so loud that it seemed at first like pure noise, only separating into definite streams of voices and words, guitars and drums, someplace later, someplace inside, after it had obliterated everything in its wake and all that was left was Here, Now . . . This was what Amanda had come looking for.

Sam's eyes wandered about, going from one white face to another, deathly white faces that emerged here and there from the blackness of their clothes, the air, the walls. They seemed oddly expressionless to him, perhaps because there were so few conversations going on. There was only this noise and Amanda, letting it in, welcoming it, wanting it even louder, faster. He watched transfixed, mute, a bystander to her pain and to her cure. As they stood side by side, drinking warm beer, he was aware too of a certain churning, a certain hum inside of her, an edgy rhythm that burned up all that entered, so that she could drink without getting drunk, look and look about without once stopping to focus, keep going, going, going without getting tired. It was part of the noise of the evening.

The club closed at four in the morning and it was only then that Sam turned to Amanda and gently asked, "Okay?"

"Okay," she said.

Outside, their ears continued to reverberate with a low electronic hum, the annoying residue of too much amplification, that rendered the city streets even quieter, even stiller. Everything they heard or saw or felt was filtered through this drone, leaving them both distanced and numb.

Amanda walked slower now, slowly back to Sam's loft. They were holding hands, their fingers integrated one by one, and neither had much interest in talking. Sam remembered how he used to listen to the crickets hum all through the night.

In bed, he lay on his back, keeping Amanda lightly in his arms, feeling the internal machinations gradually ebb as she fell into a half-sleep, emitting little moans, little sounds of struggle as she went. He pulled her in closer, and she came, but she was struggling still. Just as he was finally falling to sleep, he felt her bolt suddenly forward and he found her sitting up, tangled in a cold and sweaty confusion. Her eyes were wide and glazed and she stared at him in terror which only slowly melted into recognition. Then she fell against him, relieved. All she said was "Oh," as she wrapped herself about him, but there was a little chink, a little hole, and Sam climbed into it and they held onto each other for the rest of the night.

Throughout the next day, they both found themselves shaking their heads at odd intervals, trying to get rid of the dim ringing that hovered stubbornly in their ears.

Sam was always figuring something. He was constantly surrounded by scrawls of numbers. It was as if he found some basic reassurance in this, in the additions and subtractions and multiplications with which he covered every available surface—envelopes, book covers, napkins, whatever was at hand. "I'm surprised you don't compute on toilet paper," Amanda said.

"I've tried," Sam answered. "It's too soft. Besides, when was the last time you balanced your checkbook, 1979?"

"1978, actually. It was a very good year."

For Sam, there was always something that needed figuring—the rent, the words per page he typed, how many résumés he had sent out, how many résumés he had gotten back, his free-lance salaries, how much he spent per day. He needed to know, he always needed to know precisely where he stood.

He believed in equations, in solutions, in the laws of cause and effect. And so he made carefully constructed schedules that he adhered to with great determination, strict hourly, weekly, monthly schedules that left no room for the abstract, schedules that if religiously upheld would bring just rewards. He believed that too.

But New York was seemingly indifferent to his equations and his schedules and his laws—it had its own. It was a city of whims and meteors and it skipped wildly about his one-step-at-a-time plodding, turning around only to snicker at his logic. Still, though, it held him. Held him with its games of chance—there were so very many doors, surely behind one, perhaps the next one, if only you went on knocking . . . the glittering, seductive doors of New York. He had only to come up with a system.

On the first chilly-smelling day of autumn, Sam and Amanda wandered all afternoon from Little Italy to the Lower East Side and back down through SoHo, picking up cheeses and fruits and breads from the small stores and outdoor vendors. At each place, he talked for a few minutes with the proprietor until he felt Amanda growing impatient.

"Let's go," she said. "I'm getting cold."

Sam took off his suede baseball jacket and put it over Amanda's shoulders. "Let's just walk a little bit more, okay?"

"Okay."

She didn't mind really. Sam had a way of taking New York, dusting off the city soot that covered everything and rendered all but the most salient neon beams a uniform gray, and giving it back to her so that she could see the smaller, the softer lights. The delis that stayed open twenty-four hours and the Puerto Rican *bodegas* that sold Anacin in Spanish packages, the kids waiting on line for hours out on the street for their buzz-saw haircuts and the ladies in his neighborhood who went out for the paper in designer clothes and makeup, the little foreign movie houses that served cappuccinos instead of popcorn—these things he pointed at and said to Amanda, "Look. Would you look at this?" And so she began to find an enthusiasm that she thought she had long since lost by default.

And yet, if it was Sam who found the cheap Burmese restaurant and the free outdoor performances and then insisted on going to the top of the Empire State Building, it was Amanda who always seemed to know what the most-talked-about book would be and the most-played song and if he never quite grasped how she knew these things, he sensed that it was because the flow and the timing of the city were rooted deep within her, and it was one of the things about her that held him.

"Do you want to make soup for dinner?" Sam asked when they finally got back to Amanda's apartment, their arms sore from carrying the heavy groceries. "I know a great recipe."

Amanda laughed in amazement. "You know how to make homemade soup?"

"Sure. It's not exactly an Olympic accomplishment. Didn't your mother teach you anything?"

Amanda shook her head at the notion of her mother making homemade soup. "She's really a terrible cook."

They were standing side by side in the small kitchen now, lining up the vegetables.

"So when do I get to meet her?"

"Who?"

"Your mother."

"Why on earth would you want to do that?"

Sam laughed. "It's not such an unusual request," he said. "It seems kind of natural."

"I'm not the natural type."

For a few minutes, the only sound was the thud of two dull knives pounding into the wooden counter.

"Thinner," Sam said.

"Huh?"

"The mushrooms, you've got to make them thinner."

"Yes sir."

After dinner, as Amanda was changing clothes before they went out to an off-off-Broadway play, Sam yelled in to her, "I'd settle for your sister . . ."

"Someone already did," she yelled back.

Mabel sat at the piano with her eyes closed, humming the words she had forgotten or was too tired to sing. A long mirror was set up so that the people sitting on stools around the semicircular bar could see her hands and there was an enormous brandy snifter sitting atop the piano for tips and paid requests. Next to this was Mabel's scotch. When she opened her eyes, they formed watery red slits, slightly bored, slightly amused, weary. She was over seventy, after all.

Sam and Amanda sat in front of her and nursed their overpriced drinks. The bar had been there for years, close to the river on one of the rougher streets, and it was usually filled with men, big men, who came to see Mabel. Men liked Mabel. Paper Christmas decorations hung twelve months a year and it always seemed deep crimson inside.

"I love it here," Sam whispered in between strains of "Strange Fruit," as if thanking Amanda for a gift.

"I thought you would," Amanda said, pleased.

Their stools were close together and their legs were touching from their hipbones to their ankles—it was that kind of a place too.

About two in the morning, some musicians who had just gotten done with their own gig came around and set up a big stand-up bass and some drums behind Mabel and they slid right into a deep down sexy blues and bop riff while Mabel hummed and drank her scotch. On the next number, she stood up and passed the mike around the bar giving anyone who wished a chance to sing a line or two, as she watched, regal and bemused. Amanda put her head down shyly on Sam's shoulder when it came to her and Sam winked up at Mabel as she passed them by. He was half in love with her already; Amanda had seen it happen before. They didn't talk much, not even during the break, but they were content to be blue inside of this deep crimson place together.

"I wish I could think of a song to ask her to sing," Sam said when it was evident that the evening was closing down. He had grown up wild about the blues but now he could think of nothing. She had sung them all.

Mabel sat at her piano till a little past four and then she nodded good night to her guests and looked distantly at each of them.

"Let's give her our money," Sam said.

"How much?"

Sam was late-night drunk now and in love and the blues had turned him inside out. "All of it," he said with the enthusiasm of a convert.

"Are you serious?" Amanda asked. She knew that it wasn't the best of ideas, but it was so unlike Sam, so unlike his caution and his planning, that she was readily seduced.

"Sure," he said, and he emptied out his pockets into the brandy snifter. Amanda was laughing now and she had a newfound respect for Mabel and her power over men.

"I guess we're walking home," she said as they stepped out into the sharpness of the night.

"It's good for you." Sam put his arm around her to keep her warm. "Man, she was great."

The streets were deserted and an empty bus rattled noisily down the block. "She's too old for you," Amanda said teasingly.

"What?" He was only half listening to her anyway.

Amanda smiled. "Never mind."

"You know, you say that a lot."

"Say what a lot?"

"Never mind. You say never mind a lot." His voice was gentle and he was not knocking against her, only softly trying to slip inside.

"I guess it's usually not that important."

"Why don't you let me decide that?" For if only he could get inside, he was sure it would be crimson and blue there too. "You just don't want to let me know what you're thinking."

"Right now what I'm thinking is that I wish we had cab fare."

Sam laughed and pulled her in tighter. They still had seventeen blocks to go.

He stood at the door in his jacket and tie, his hands behind his back, grinning like a schoolboy. Amanda kissed him hello and he came in and handed her a large bouquet of flowers. Yellow and pink ribbons trailed happily from the ends. She blushed when she opened the paisley paper and found a dozen rich red tulips inside.

"What's the occasion?" she asked.

"No occasion."

Amanda was wearing a short black velvet skirt and a white velvet top with a hundred tiny buttons down the front and Sam undid the first four and slipped his hand inside. He kissed the nape of her neck and he began to enclose her but she slid away from him. "I'd better put these in water," she said softly and she went into the kitchen and cut off the tulips' ends and mashed them and put pennies in the water—all supposed to make them open, make them last. Sam stood in the doorway watching her, amused and touched by her embarrassment.

"I'll just go put these inside and then we can get going," Amanda said.

"What's your rush?"

Amanda stopped and looked at Sam curiously for a moment, looked at his eagerness and his grin and his obvious desire, and she wondered what was going on. It was as if he had come to some sort of decision about her while she wasn't paying attention.

"I thought you wanted to go to this party."

"I see the people from *Backlog* too much as it is. Besides, I thought you liked being fashionably late."

He followed her as she put the flowers on the nightstand and then he pulled her down onto the bed. She lay still and watched him as he took off her top, her skirt, her patterned stockings, watched his avid smile and traced it with her fingertips. And then she was above him, untying his tie, unbuttoning his shirt, and he watched her, her veiled eyes serious and lovely. They made love as they never quite had before—as if they meant it—seeking out the hollows and the hardnesses that were theirs alone.

It was early evening and they lay in the stillness, their bodies lightly grazing each other. "You don't like the people you work with, do you?" Amanda asked.

"I didn't say I don't like them. We just don't have that much in common."

"Neither do we," Amanda said, and it was a question, really.

Sam reached down and kissed her breast playfully. "Sure we do."

They lay quietly, lazily, hiding from the rest of the night.

"Amanda?"

"Yes?"

"Wasn't there ever anything you wanted to do?" He had wanted to ask her this before, but he was fearful that she would turn away from him, annoyed, sarcastic. "Even when you were younger?"

"All I can ever remember wanting to do was get out," Amanda said. She ran her finger up and down the long muscle of Sam's forearm. "I guess I didn't stop to figure out what I would do once I got there. Then it just seemed like it was too late to want anything in particular."

"Why was it too late?"

"I don't know. It just was. You're very lucky, knowing what you want."

Sam didn't say anything.

In a little while, they picked their clothes up off the floor and they started out all over again.

The party was in honor of the latest *Backlog* cover girl and the bar where it was being held was crammed with models and musicians and reporters who pretended to be both. Amanda held on to Sam's hand through most of the evening, surprised by how many people he knew. And if she didn't pay much attention to whom she was being introduced, it was only because she was absorbed by how nonchalantly they accepted her as Sam's girlfriend. Sam's girlfriend. His hand was firm and dry in hers.

They went to sleep quite late that night and Sam only kissed her gently on the forehead and said, "Sweet dreams." And Amanda thought, well maybe this is it, maybe I can have it after all, maybe this is it. But all she said was, "Good night, Sam."

"She's going deaf, you know," Sally yelled into the kitchen where Amanda was dripping coffee for them. "She won't admit it, but I'm sure she is."

"I think she hears what she wants to hear." Amanda came in and put a mug next to her sister. "Don't look for a problem where there isn't one," she said.

"You never see a problem anyplace."

They were not getting off on the right foot, not at all. Sally had called up wanting a conference—What do we do about Mother?—she had called up wanting commiseration and a mutual female indignation, not a lecture from her oh-so-levelheaded sister. In fact, they had both been taking baby steps toward each other lately, trying to wobble around the lines and the rules, trying not to follow every inch forward with the usual retreat.

Sally sat on one of the small wooden chairs in Amanda's living room, wondering when she planned on buying some furniture. Aside from these rather quirky old school chairs, which Amanda had painted in deep glossy jewel tones, soothing underwater colors, her apartment was virtually bare. The black and white asymmetrical shelves that she had designed and built herself remained largely empty, barren of the little mementos with which most people comfort themselves. There were no two cups that matched, no two plates. She had painted the floors battleship gray when she had first moved in three years ago and promptly forgotten about any more domestic touches. Sally looked around with customary annoyance, wondering just where Amanda thought she was going to pick up and run to. But she wouldn't say anything. Not today.

"She hardly ever leaves the apartment," Sally continued.

Amanda had also gotten flashes of her mother—watching the news, drinking her sherry, feeding the twenty-year-old Persian cat, images of her mother, alone, and they caught her up short. "Maybe she could get a job," she said. "Or do some volunteer work. Who knows, maybe she'll even meet a new man."

"I did mention the idea of a part-time job to her," Sally said in between quick sips of her coffee. "But I don't think she took it too seriously. What in God's name would she do, anyway?"

They had more coffee and they tried to devise little schemes to get their mother out of the house but they were desultory efforts for neither of them really believed that she would ever be anything other than Mrs. Easton, at home, alone.

Amanda waited for Sally to leave but she didn't seem to be doing that and so they talked of other things. Frank's name came up of course, but it had long been accepted that he and Amanda didn't like each other and she tensed when Sally mentioned him. It had something to do with the way he sat back and bit his lip, always judging, never approving. He was possessed with a rigid morality, a finely honed indignation that had burst forth at Amanda more than once. She had watched too as he grilled Sally about the ingredients in the bread she bought and lectured about the proper exercise and scraped the salt off the tops of crackers—he knew all about what was right and good. And if they came to the edge of an argument in Amanda's presence, Sally quickly backed off, claiming love as she went.

Sally ate another of the cookies Amanda had put out. "Frank wants another baby," she said flatly.

"Do you?"

"Of course I do," Sally answered quickly. "I just wanted to wait a little longer, that's all."

"Then why don't you?"

"I don't know. It seems kind of selfish, I guess. He's desperate for a son."

Amanda stood up and her voice came out harsher than she had meant. "I think you should wait until you're ready."

"It's not that simple," Sally snapped. "You don't understand the first thing about marriage."

Amanda lit a cigarette and laughed sarcastically because she knew it would annoy her sister. "Well then why don't you explain it to me? What's the first thing about marriage?"

Sally looked at her for a moment and felt suddenly too tired for this. She grabbed another cookie and she laughed. "Missionary position on a Saturday night—that's what marriage is." The two sisters looked at each other in mutual surprise, and delight, just the way they had when they were kids and one of them had dared to use a naughty word.

But when Sally put on her coat to leave, she said, "Forget I said that. We really do have a perfect marriage. It's just the weather turning and Maggie's teething and . . . It's nothing. Really."

"Last chance," Amanda said. "You sure you don't want to stay at one of those places with a heart-shaped tub?"

Sam kept his eyes on the road. "Nope," he said. "I told you, I want to see some of your East Coast charm. Shingles, beaches . . ."

"You mean we're going for quaint here?"

"You got it."

"Well keep in mind we're headed for the Hamptons."

Except for the back of a cab, Sam and Amanda had never been in a car together before and they sat far apart in the front seat of the rented Chevrolet, caught off guard by the closed window, closed-in intimacy of driving on a windy morning. Sam's hand rested confidently on the wheel, steady and in control, and gradually Amanda began to edge closer to his side.

It was midafternoon when they pulled up in front of an old Victorian lady of a hotel, but it was off season and it was easy to get a room for the night. It was all so easy, checking in, chatting with the woman who showed them upstairs, closing the door behind her, as if they were a couple who did this sort of thing all the time—Let's get away for the weekend, dear—that Sam and Amanda both felt somewhat like impostors.

They put their small canvas bags down and looked about the room. There was a large four-poster bed covered with a thick down quilt of snowy white and there were faded multicolored braided rugs scattered about the mahogany floors, there was a fireplace with three sturdy logs lying in wait . . . Amanda walked over to the window and pulled the heavy drapes aside and looked out on the empty duck pond, dark emerald green and forbidding.

In a minute, Sam came over and put his arms around her. "Do you want to go check out the beach?" he asked.

"Sure, just give me a minute." Amanda went into the bathroom and washed off all of her makeup and changed her boots to sneakers. "Let's go," she said, coming out and heading for the door.

They parked the car in the deserted lot of the main public beach and left their shoes behind as they walked to the shore, the sand cold and damp between their toes. The ocean was short choppy stripes of gray and white and the water was far too icy to touch but it was as if years of sweet suntan lotion had settled into the sand and they could almost smell it as they walked in their bundles of sweaters, their arms about each other's waists.

"I used to dream about the ocean when I was a kid," Sam said. "It was a great mystery to me."

"Did you dream of running away to sea, leaving a lady in every port?"

"Only for a week or two."

The houses were huge and empty and ominous, full of gables and glass and summer ghosts as they walked on and on.

"I used to dream of the ocean too," Amanda said.

"What about it?"

"Well, Dr. Freud, I used to have recurring dreams about tidal waves. Of being swallowed up, drowning."

Sam didn't say anything but only pulled her closer, closer and up, until they were in the dunes, the long sparse blades of grass tickling their hands, and then they were down, laughing and rolling over and over and the clammy sand stuck to their fingers, their cheeks, their hair. "Let me get on top," Amanda said and it was shivering and cold and they held each other tight.

As they drove back into town they sat very close to each other and Amanda rested her head in the hollow of Sam's neck, tired and content. They stopped for dinner at a local restaurant, the seafood special, and then they went back to the hotel.

There was a fire going in their room and someone had turned the bed down and there was no place they would rather be. Sam turned on the radio, moving the dial patiently up and down until he found a station nestled amid the static. "Chances are," Johnny Mathis quavered, " 'Cause I wear a silly grin, the moment you come into view . . ."

He turned around and held his hand out to Amanda. "Care to dance?" he asked, bowing slightly.

She looked at his hand for a moment and then looked away. "C'mon," she said, laughing apprehensively.

"Don't worry, Amanda, no one's going to see you."

His hand was still out and she took it and they moved slowly about the room, her hand playing in his hair, damp and thickened by the ocean air, his lips on her cheek, soft and salty, and Johnny faded in and out, "Chances are your chances are awfully good . . ."

"Ouch," Sam said when Amanda stepped on his foot for the fifth time. "For a thin girl you're awfully heavy on your feet."

She pulled away, embarrassed. "Sorry," she said testily. "I don't know how to dance like this."

Sam put his arm firmly about her and pulled her back. "You're just too stiff," he said. "You've got to relax and stop anticipating."

Amanda concentrated on relaxing, letting her spine soften and soften and slowly she melted into his lead and then she melted more.

They were deep beneath the thick down quilt when the singing stopped and the news came on and the fire sputtered noisily down.

Amanda woke up first the next morning and snuggled closer to Sam. When she felt him gradually waken, she whispered softly, "I wish we could stay another day."

"I know. Me too. But I've got to get back."

Amanda pulled away so slightly that she could have claimed not to but she did and he knew that she did. "We'll come back another time," he said.

"Sure."

They stayed in bed a little longer, reluctant to leave the room behind, but their minds were already climbing into their city clothes.

They were quiet on the ride back, playing with the radio and listening to the highway go by beneath them as the rows and rows of houses grew closer together and they passed the empty fairgrounds. They both grew edgy as the skyline suddenly sprouted before them and the air was no longer fresh.

"It always looks so dirty when you come back," Amanda said.

"You make it sound as if we were gone for months."

"I wish," she muttered.

"No you don't," he said. "Not really."

She said nothing.

Sam honked the horn angrily when they got stuck behind a cab on Second Avenue. "Why don't I just drop you off?" he said. "There's no reason you have to return the car with me."

"You sure?"

"Sure."

When they got to her door, he reached in the back where her bag was waiting and handed it to her. "I'll call you later," he said. They sat in the car for a moment, the motor going, wanting to separate, not wanting to separate, there was that room . . .

"Bye," Amanda said finally, and they gave each other a brief staccato kiss.

Amanda had trouble falling asleep that night and she curled up in the corner of the bed and kicked angrily at the sheets, trying to escape the grains of sand she had brought home with her, winter sand.

Patrick, the managing editor of *Backlog,* called Sam into his office. His dark brown hair was falling across his eyes and his Armani clothes were properly wrinkled and as always, he looked amiable and harried and vacuous. Sam spent a good deal of time wondering if there was more or less to him than met the eye.

"You've been doing good work," he said to Sam as he looked down at some layouts that Sam had had nothing to do with.

"Thanks."

"I think it's time you tried something new."

"I'd like that," Sam said.

"How about doing some record reviews?"

Sam had hoped for more than this. "I don't really know all that much about music," he said.

Patrick looked up and smiled. "Neither do the people making it."

Sam shifted his weight from one foot to the other. "How about something else?" he asked.

"Okay. There's this. We're starting a new feature, maybe you heard—Hunk of the Month. How'd you like a shot at the first one?"

Sam took the subway to the Upper East Side where

he had arranged to meet March's hunk—a Swedish actor who had been in a couple of porno flicks and had somehow landed a role in a big Hollywood epic. Sam saw him from the window outside the restaurant—it had to be him—an enormous blond warship of a man dressed all in white.

The actor spoke very little English and there was a dull film over his eyes, like dirty cellophane, and yet he tried so hard, his huge square chin thrust forward, toward Sam, straining to understand.

"So how did you find your Hollywood experience?" Sam asked.

"It was okay." The actor leaned forward on his massive arms. "But I do theater next. Serious theater."

"I see," Sam said. "Well. Do you like being a sex symbol?"

"I told you," the actor replied, frowning. "I'm serious. Not symbol. Serious actor."

"Of course." Sam smiled politely and wrote "serious" down on his pad in large letters so that the actor could see that he got the point.

They continued this way for a half hour or so until they were both satisfied that they had covered every possible base and then they sat back and ordered some beers. They stayed together for another hour, looking out the window and commenting, more with sounds than words, on the meticulously dressed women and the important-looking men who passed by, and sometimes they just sat in a congenial silence.

Suddenly, the actor glanced at his Rolex watch and stood up in a hurry. He smacked Sam firmly on the back. "Thank you for the media attention," he said and he put on his sunglasses and left.

It took Sam less than forty-five minutes that night to write up the interview. He titled it "But Seriously, Folks . . ." and then he proofread it hastily before allowing himself to take out all three of the city papers he had picked up on the way home. He read up on the latest city corruption scandal—how far up it would go and who had told the most outrageous lies and what the price might be and he rewrote each story in his mind—this is how I would do it, if only I could do it, what if I never get to do it?

Patrick called Sam at home two days later.

"Just wanted to let you know," he said. "I really like what you did with that piece."

"Thanks."

"The Hunk of the Month column . . ." Patrick paused for dramatic effect. "It's yours."

Sam said thank you and hung up the phone.

Amanda called Sam early in the afternoon.

"Are you doing anything tonight?" she asked.

"No. What's up?"

"Well, Sally thought maybe we could come over for dinner. We don't have to if you don't want to, I mean I really don't want to, I just thought . . ."

"Amanda, you know I'd love to."

"I was afraid of that."

"What time should I pick you up?"

"Six-thirty."

Sam and Amanda sat at the long rectangular table alone. Sally was in the kitchen putting the finishing touches on the main course and Frank was putting Maggie down for the night. The lacquered chairs had high straight backs forcing them to sit up so stiffly that it reminded Sam of church.

"Nice china," Sam said when the four of them were finally seated. It was an ornate pattern of burgundy and gold.

"One of the benefits of getting married," Sally said and Amanda shifted position, feeling immediately that they were approaching dangerous ground.

Frank sat at the head of the table with a paternal air

and conducted the conversation with a carefully constructed politeness.

"You're in the newspaper business, right?" he asked.

"Right," Sam said, smiling broadly. "And you?"

"Public relations."

"Shocking but true," Amanda interjected. Everyone ignored her.

Sam began to ask Frank about the specifics of his job and he complimented Sally on her raspberry chicken and he was the first to stand up and help clear the dishes and all the time, Amanda sat still, making eye contact with no one.

When Sam excused himself for a moment, Sally turned to Amanda and exclaimed, "I like him. I really like him. And Frank does too. Don't you, honey?"

"He's so normal," Frank said, sounding more than a little surprised.

"What did you think, I only go out with psychotics?"

Sally gave her husband a sharp look. "Well," Frank grumbled, "it would certainly be unique if you work it out."

"Unique?"

Sam came back to the table just in time. "I think I'll go check on Maggie," Frank said, standing up.

"No, I'll go," Amanda volunteered.

She walked down the hallway lined with family photographs and quietly pushed open the door to the nursery. It was dark and still inside and the only light came from Maggie's huge eyes, staring hopefully at Amanda. She was sitting up in her crib and the red wool hair of her Raggedy Ann was caught up in her mouth.

Amanda smiled and lifted her out of the crib, kissing her wispy yellow hair and whispering hello. Even when there was no one to see, she could not bring herself to use a baby voice, but nevertheless, she spoke so gently and playfully that Maggie's face lit up with delight. She sat down cross-legged on the floor and propped Maggie up facing her.

They sat for a moment smiling idiotically at each other and then Maggie raised her sausage arm and tugged cheerfully at Amanda's lips. Her fingers were firm and the knuckles were like little puddles in the soft ball of flesh and Amanda pretended to nibble at her hand.

"Why don't the two of us run away together?" Amanda asked.

Maggie nodded her head and smiled.

"A deserted island? The tropics?"

Maggie leaned up against her aunt, watching her intently.

"I know, I know, your tastes run more to Disneyland. I don't see why we couldn't stop off there for a day or two before we . . ."

She noticed that Maggie's eyes were focused on the door now and she followed her gaze to where Sam was standing, smiling down at them.

"How long have you been there?" Amanda asked.

"Just a couple of minutes."

"Oh. Well. She was awake, so I just thought, anyway, I guess I should put her back to bed."

Sam watched as Amanda stood up and put Maggie back in her crib. "Don't forget," she whispered and kissed her on the forehead.

Sam took her hand as they walked down the hallway.

"Let's go soon," Amanda said. "Okay?"

"Definitely."

And they went back to the dining room, where Sally had coffee and dessert waiting for them.

They had reached the point where they no longer needed the multitude of excuses the city had to offer for lovers to meet. They decided to try spending an evening in, alone, with nothing planned. "Another hot date," Amanda said to Nancy. "One more exciting evening." But there was a clear undertone of pride and pleasure lighting up her voice, there was no real boredom or frustration. For this was a line she had rarely crossed before, this first step in the loosening of facades.

On her way home from work, Amanda stopped to pick up some Cokes and cheese and crackers and ice cream. The first time Sam had looked in her refrigerator, he had said, "You sure must eat out a lot." He had gotten used to it by now, the assortment of wilted carrots and stale bread and wine that had been uncorked months ago, and he had gotten used to trips to the corner pizza shop. "But Christ," he would say, "don't you even have a Coke?"

Now Amanda carried home the groceries with a secret delight, as if they were pornography, sex tools to be used in the night ahead. Shopping for her man. She even caught herself smiling as she put them away, though she turned her mouth back down immediately.

They settled in comfortably, having decided somewhat self-consciously to each go about their business as if this were business as usual. Amanda watched a made-for-TV movie about a lawyer who ran off with her death-row client while Sam leafed through the book he had brought over. "You can't go wrong with Huckleberry Finn," he said, and as a sign of how close and comfortable they were, they set out to ignore each other.

Amanda was having trouble following the plot though. She stared at disparate images on the screen and she could not seem to keep track of who was good, who was bad. "I bought you some Cokes," she said finally, keeping her eyes on the television.

Sam looked up from his book. He knew this was something. "You're kidding me," he said, and gave her hand a little squeeze.

On his way back from the refrigerator, Sam stopped to look out the window. "He's back," he yelled in to Amanda. Every night at precisely seven o'clock a tattered man appeared at the phone booth outside. He would pick up the receiver and begin to chant, slamming the phone into its cradle in perfect rhythm with his angry, indecipherable prayers, over and over and over again. At exactly nine o'clock, he would leave as purposefully as he had come. Sam and Amanda had come to refer to him as "our bum" the way other lovers had "our song."

"Our bum's back," Sam said. "Can you hear him?" But something in him shrank as he said it and the sound of Amanda's ready laughter only made it worse. It just didn't taste right.

Later, Sam put away his book and they ate the ice cream and watched *Nightline*. Every now and then, he let go of loud and conscious yawns. "I'm bushed," he said, and Amanda laughed at this too, for she knew it was his way of saying, Not tonight, and it was the only reaction she could summon. He kissed her chastely and went to sleep, while she lay awake, wanting him and wounded.

In the morning, when he kissed her, when he curled around her and squeezed her breast, she was flooded again by this want, a tingling liquid heat. But when he got out of bed abruptly and started to dress, she did not say, "Come back. Hold me. Make love to me." She did not know how.

"To work," Sam said cheerfully, and let himself out.

She had gotten three letters from her father in the last two weeks and she sat with them before her. The first two were long letters, at least five pages each, tracking skeins of disappointments, grabbing at past incidents and trying to pin them down under a bright light to finally examine them. Explain them. Apologize for them. And dismiss them. Amanda gathered that this effort had something to do with his new therapy, his new lady . . .

And so he skipped from one depressingly standard alcoholic failing to the next, gathering handfuls of blame as he went. The missed dates and the maudlin jags, the grandiose promises, the lies—"I was sick then," he said. "I'm recovering now. Surely you'll give me one more chance, darling?" But his letters also reflected the black holes that he could not apologize for or explain, for he did not remember them, and the specifics of these episodes remained etched into her like a tattoo where he had only blackness and amnesia.

Amanda lit another cigarette. She remembered the time he had broken a particularly hopeful spell of sobriety and he found her pouring what was left of his whiskey down the kitchen sink. It was the only time he had ever hit her. His raised hand, his animal face—that moment was frozen inside of her, for something had died then. There had been no more yelling after that, no more pleading or strikes or even silent prayers. She had walked away holding her cheek and she did not say a word. For days afterward, he kept asking her what was wrong.

"You understand, you forgive me," the second letter ended. "Please say you do. Whatever I did, I always loved you."

When she was a teenager, Amanda had heard that alcoholism is an often inherited disease and she used to wait for the morning when she would wake up ill with it. And when it did not come to her, she began to court it, tempting it out of its lair, daring it to take her. She drank rum-and-Cokes out of soda cans in the high school cafeteria and she went out for too many whiskey sours with boys just old enough to sneak her into bars and she went to sleep more than once clutching the sheets for balance. But she did not become an alcoholic and she was not any closer to understanding why her father was and so she put it aside. There were other things.

The third letter, the one that had come this morning, was shorter. "Dearest," he wrote, "my dearest Amanda. The wedding is set for next month, but due to a variety of family matters, we are planning to go by ourselves to the local Justice. Joan's sister will stand up for us. I realize that you will probably not want to come. But darling, it would mean so much to me, and to Joan, to know that we had your blessing."

Amanda sat and let the living room go gray with the late afternoon. One way or another, she would have to give him her blessing. She was his favorite. But he had long ago taken a hammer to her special love for him and shattered it into a thousand shards and she could not give it back whole to him, not even if she had wanted to.

She got up and switched on the lights. Early on, Amanda had learned this trick: make up a mood. Make up a mood and then just be it. It usually worked. Tonight, she would be sweet and slow.

Nancy and Amanda were in the ladies' room, leaning up against the cool tile and taking surreptitious looks into the mirror while they waited their turns.

"You're so nice to him," Nancy said.

"Why do you sound so surprised? Of course I'm nice to him. What's the matter, don't you think I'm a nice person?"

"Of course I do. It's just that, I don't know—you're usually so sarcastic about Sam. I'm just surprised to see how well behaved you're being. Almost deferential."

"Oh c'mon."

When they got back to the table, Jack and Sam were having an enthusiastic conversation about the fine art of knuckleballs and they only grudgingly gave this up for a more general topic. They ordered their dinners and more beers and they separated into various twos, men and women, couple and couple, and diagonally across too, and then they came up and they were four again. The meal took a long time coming and as they ordered yet another round of Dos Equis, Amanda relaxed and thought, well yes, this is working just fine, and she watched as Sam eased into it too.

Jack began to describe a case he was working on for

the city. Every now and then, he wandered into some technicality that no one grasped, but Nancy pulled him back and he answered their questions patiently because he wanted them to see, really see, how important it was that they got this scumbag. His enthusiasm was infectious and soon they were all raising their beer bottles and toasting the scumbag's demise.

The Cajun food was hot and it made them drink quickly and redden. Sam was obviously having a good time and Amanda liked watching him, liked seeing the way his cheeks folded in and his eyes creased when he smiled. And Sam liked watching Amanda too, seeing how comfortable she was with these old friends, how easily she accepted being teased and prodded and how readily she gave it back.

Nancy was talking now about Legacies, about how good business was and how good Amanda was at it. "You'd be surprised," she said, "but she really has a very good head for business."

"You're right," Sam said. "I would be surprised." Amanda hit him.

"I keep telling her that I want to make her a full-time partner. I'm really going to need someone once I have a kid."

This was the first Sam had heard of this proposal and he was surprised that Amanda hadn't mentioned it to him. Her look said, not now, though and after a moment of discomfort, the subject changed.

"So what kind of writing do you do?" Jack asked.

"Fashion reporting, mostly," Sam said, his eyes on the greasy tablecloth. "Performance reviews, sometimes some interviews."

"'Is that what you did before you came to New York?"

Sam laughed. "Well Allensville is not exactly known for its performance clubs, but the carnivals and bazaars were better training ground than I realized."

"What made you decide to come here anyway?" Nancy asked.

"Lately I've been trying to remember that myself." He was not laughing as much as before.

Amanda looked at Sam with real surprise. "I didn't realize you were so unhappy here."

"I'm not. It's just that sometimes I think I came here too late. Maybe it's easier if you come here when you're twenty-one. I don't know, I always feel one step behind."

"It takes time," Nancy said.

Amanda said nothing.

Nancy and Jack were uneasy witnesses to these ellipses and discoveries and they were anxious to get back onto safer footing. They embarked on a loud political argument with all four of them interrupting each other, trying to make a crucial point, when they finally stopped and realized that they were all making the same point and they had to laugh. Before they left Jack and Sam made arrangements to go to a Knicks game together.

As they walked home arm in arm, tightened by the display of others' disparities, Jack turned to Nancy and asked, "What on earth do you think they talk about?"

Outside of Sam's window there was a cracked-up white Porsche. The left side was all folded into itself and the front window was a catastrophe of shattered glass. The hood was permanently raised into a painful snarl. One of the first things he did every morning was look to see what latest insult the night had brought. First the tires were taken one by one. Then the steering wheel. One morning, dripping red graffiti had appeared on the back end. Still, underneath it all, there lurked a gorgeous white Porsche, a satin couple with streaming hair at the wheel—that's what he thought, anyway, and other people must have thought so too because so many stopped to look and to touch it.

This morning, he peered through the venetian blinds to catch up on its progress and he stayed there, looking out at the street. He was not wearing a shirt, just his meticulously faded jeans, and the cold glass pane against his forehead made him shiver, but still, he stayed there. He had nothing much else to do but watch the trucks rattling toward the tunnel and the women with their strollers. He had plenty of time.

After a while, he got dressed and went to the local Ukrainian diner for the $1.99 breakfast special, reading the *Times,* by-line by by-line, while he ate. He had a third cup of coffee while he did what he could of the crossword puzzle and then he put it aside to banter with his favorite waitress, the one with the bright red beehive and the maternal padding about her waist and the old Ukrainian slippers that looked like toeless sneakers. For some reason, she had taken to calling him Sammy. "Ven you gonna git yourself a decent job, Sammy?" she asked pleasantly. Sam smiled sheepishly. The last of his job applications had been politely refused yesterday.

When it was almost noon, he walked over to *Backlog*'s offices, hoping that they would be open by now. A few of the more ambitious staff were just beginning to straggle in with their take-out coffee cups and their omnipresent hangovers and their rivers of gossip from the night before. Sam wasn't in the mood to talk to them and he picked up the passes for the evening's assignment with as little involvement as possible. "It's going to be fabulous," Patrick reassured him. "*The* designer to watch. And the club, well fabulous is really the only word, but you already knew that."

The club was an enormous cavern left over from another era, vast and still gilt-edged in places, though now it was decorated with the latest in neo-expressionist art. There was level upon level of lights and sculptures and people, hordes of people filling in the crevices. Sam and Amanda stood on the third-floor balcony and looked down at the dance floor. As they watched the single people, the twos and the threes, gyrating, an enormous cityscape descended from the ceiling onto the floor. The dancers hardly noticed as they fitted themselves about it.

"Fabulous," Sam said dryly.

Amanda looked at him and laughed curiously.

The show was supposed to start at twelve, but it was

past one A.M. when the models finally took to the stage. The cardboard city was pulled up and replaced by a huge lime green neon dollar sign and "Puttin' on the Ritz" replaced Top-40. The first man out had hair below his shoulders and was wearing an oversized shiny zoot suit in turquoise flecked with black. He laughed and waved to his friends in the audience as he ripped up the paper money that was crammed into his suit pockets, gleefully throwing shreds of bills up in the air. Gentleman after gentleman pranced out, some with eye patches, some with martini glasses, some with high-top sneakers, all with brilliant shining suits, large shoulder pads, and wads of money to shower on the adoring crowd.

Sam and Amanda stood on chair tops, craning to see. "Who do they think is going to wear these things?" Sam asked. "I don't know," Amanda said. "I think I'd look pretty good in that pink one." Sam looked to see if she was kidding but he didn't think she was. He tried to take notes but the girl next to him kept knocking her elbow into his pad. They had long since been separated from the photographer assigned with him. "Wide shoulders," Sam kept repeating to himself. "Wide shoulders, wide shoulders . . ."

It was two in the morning and Sam was in a horrendous mood. Two in the morning and he was in a fucking dolled-up airplane hangar crammed with people who did not talk to each other, taking notes on a bunch of faggots in clown costumes. And this was the hot ticket in New York. He looked over to see that Amanda was laughing and cheering along with the rest of the crowd.

The designer came out and was heartily congratulated and then the models and the dollar sign and the smooth sounds vanished and it was back to business as usual. He and Amanda tried to dance but the floor was so crowded that it was impossible for them to raise their arms. It didn't matter, the night had already gone good and sour.

"What are you going to write about it?" Amanda asked on the way home.

"That it was a bunch of well-dressed souls flitting about Hades."

"I don't think that's quite what they're looking for."

He pulled the blinds up all the way so that the early morning light banged at Amanda's eyes. She covered her head with a pillow and muttered, "Do you have to do that?" But she knew that he did. He continued to wake with an energy that she could only ascribe to his Midwestern upbringing. There was no other way that she could attempt to forgive his immediate desire for light, for movement, for the day.

He brought her coffee in bed and she took blind sips while he dressed, shuffled his papers about, went down to check the mail—the impatient sounds of a morning person. When he came back he found her lying bare-breasted with her dark shades on. Even beneath her sunglasses, her eyes were closed.

"You look like an O.D.'d movie star," he said.

She didn't answer. Sam sat down on the edge of the bed and opened his mail. Inside of a pink scented envelope there was a long letter and a large bunch of Polaroids. He skimmed the tiny handwriting and began to examine the pictures, smiling at each one and then passing it to Amanda.

There was a fat, slatternly woman in the first one, smiling broadly and squinting into the sun. Her white hair was cropped short and she was wearing a flowered housedress with a single ruffle at the bottom. Behind her, with his arm around his wife's shoulder, was Sam's father, a thin, balding man in a plaid shirt, a proud man. "They look very nice," Amanda said, handing the photo back to Sam. The mothers in her world were all trim and well preserved. For many, in fact, preservation was their sole occupation.

The next pictures were of Sam's nieces and nephews. With their sturdy legs and incredible towheads, no children had ever seemed quite that young or that healthy before. "My sister just had another baby," Sam said. "But I guess they knew better than to send me the infant pictures." Underneath the bravado there was a whiff of disappointment, and though he made a few more disparaging remarks, they had no edge.

He wanted her to leave. He wanted to look at the pictures slowly, alone. He got up and put them away in his desk drawer.

"Can you throw me a cigarette?" Amanda yelled to him. She was still wearing her sunglasses.

Her smoking had never really bothered him before, but now, this morning, the way it smelled and tasted and looked, it did. It bothered him immensely.

"The first words out of your mouth in the delivery room won't be is it a boy or girl but can I have a cigarette."

Amanda sat up. "Excuse me? What delivery room is it you're referring to? Do you know something I don't know?"

"Oh forget it. Here." He threw her the pack of cigarettes and pulled out what few notes he had taken the night before. He sat at his desk, chewing the end of his pencil and waiting for Amanda to leave.

Amanda put on her clothes, her makeup. She went

over to the desk and when he did not turn around, she kissed the top of his head. "Good-bye," she said.

"Bye. I'll call you later."

She made her way home through the bright morning to shower and change before going to work.

Sam took out the photographs as soon as she left. He read his mother's news of home and tried to work but he couldn't. Finally, he pulled out his dark gray stationery from the bottom drawer. "Dear Cathy," he wrote to his ex-girlfriend, "I know you probably don't want to hear from me, but . . ."

The invitation said "Black Tie," and they threw everything they could find that was black and sequined and shiny onto the bed.

"Are you sure you wouldn't rather take Jack?" Amanda asked.

"Are you kidding? He can't stand this kind of thing."

Nancy rotated slowly so that Amanda could pin a hem on the black crepe pants that she hadn't had time to finish.

"There," Amanda said proudly. "Finished."

Nancy looked in the mirror and saw that her pants were at least ten different lengths.

"Okay, so I'm bad at this sort of thing," Amanda said impatiently as she stood up. "Why don't you just borrow a skirt? We're already an hour late as it is."

They continued to pick up one shimmery article after another, velvets bought on sale and thrift-shop taffetas and heavily beaded cardigans, taking off, putting on, vamping—a bebopaloo cartoon version of glamour.

"What's this party for, anyway?" Amanda asked as they searched for a cab.

"Oh I don't know. Some dead American artist. It'll be fun though. I've never been to one of these really chichi museum affairs."

Nancy took the number of limos parked outside to be a very good sign and she hurriedly paid the driver and gave him a magnanimous tip. But once inside, the crowd was sparser than she had expected and only occasionally in Black Tie.

"We look better than anyone here," she said with more disappointment than pride.

They wandered about the large gray rooms, looking at the colorful precisionist paintings and the stark black-and-white photographs, and looking too for champagne, but there was none. Only a cash bar.

"Now that's tacky," Nancy said disgustedly. "Let's go someplace where we'll be appreciated."

The two headed up Madison Avenue in their short velvet skirts and their high heels and went into the Carlyle Hotel, entering one of the smaller saloons. Clustered at small round tables about the piano were numerous couples, the women in silk dresses and gold earrings and straight shoulder-length hair, the men in dark business suits. Amanda and Nancy made their way past them and settled at the bar.

Like all hotel bars, even the dark and rich and expensive ones, there were drifts of melancholy, and they drank their wine in silence while a woman in a polka dot dress crooned softly about the man who done her wrong.

"So how's your sister?" Nancy asked during a break. "Is she knocked up yet?"

Amanda sat up straighter. "What?"

Nancy sighed. "God, I'm sorry," she said. "That was awful. It's just that . . . Well, to tell you the truth, I hate pregnant women. Really. Every place I go lately, I see pregnant women and I want to punch them in the face." Nancy's voice cracked and her shoulders shook with quivers and gasps. Amanda put her hand tentatively on her forearm and then moved it to her back, rubbing it gently up and down.

"I'm sorry," Nancy said. She bit her lip and sniffed. "I'm okay now. Really." Amanda put her hands back on the bar.

"You want to hear something really crazy?" Nancy kept her eyes on the white shadows of light dancing sinuously in her wine. "Lately when I go to the supermarket, I walk up and down the aisle with all those big boxes of Pampers, wondering if I'll ever get to buy them. Pretty pathetic, huh?"

"Oh Nancy. Just be patient."

Nancy turned sharply to Amanda. "Goddammit, I'm sick of being told to be patient."

"Sorry."

Now Nancy reached to her. "No. I'm sorry. Let's just drop it."

They ordered some more wine and again listened to the singer and the bartender's prattle with the fat man next to them and the light laughter and applause of the couples at the round tables.

"You're being awfully quiet tonight," Nancy said finally. "What's going on?"

"It's Sam, I guess," Amanda said.

"What's the problem?"

"I don't know. Maybe it's nothing. We just seem kind of sick of each other, that's all."

"That's all?" Nancy laughed.

"Christ," Amanda said, dismissing the subject. "I'm tired of the whole damn thing. What I really want is a good meaningless affair."

They motioned for the check and as they waited for the bartender to ring it up, Nancy thought she might as well try to get an answer out of Amanda. "I suppose this isn't a good time to ask about the store?"

"No."

"No this isn't a good time or no you don't want the partnership?"

"No this isn't a good time."

"Let me know when it is, okay?"

"Sure. Let's get out of here."

Nancy went back to Amanda's to pick up her clothes and the two of them sat up till one in the morning, poring over Christmas catalogs and gossiping.

"By the way," Amanda said as Nancy was finally getting ready to leave. "My sister's not pregnant. Believe it or not, she's actually thinking of going back to work."

Nancy smiled and kissed Amanda good night.

For years, whenever Amanda had imagined lovers, intimacies, all she could see was this: arguing, scenes, disharmonies, and finally, silence. It was all she could see.

But she and Sam did not argue, had never once argued. Instead, they went round and round and round, dancing the minuet, porcelain figures who rarely broke their painted-on smiles.

"So what do you want to do Friday night?" Sam asked. It was no longer a question of whether or not they would see each other. It was taken for granted, neither could see a choice.

"I don't know," Amanda said. "Whatever you want to do."

Friday night came and when they spoke at six o'clock, they still had not made any plans. "Well what are Nancy and Jack doing?" Sam asked.

"They're busy," Amanda said. "Don't you have any friends we could go out with?"

"I've checked. They're all busy."

"You mean we're stuck with each other?"

"Looks that way." They both laughed uneasily. "I'll cook dinner," Sam said.

When Amanda showed up at his door a couple of hours later in thick white jogging shoes, Sam snickered in surprise. "Those don't look like quite your style," he said as he closed the door behind her.

"They're not. But I have about ten blisters on each foot at the moment."

"What happened?"

"You know those new turquoise shoes I was wearing the other day? That's what happened. They looked so innocent. A hundred bucks and I can't even walk in them."

Sam looked at her incredulously. "You spent one hundred dollars on a pair of everyday shoes?"

"That's what they cost these days."

"Are you serious?" His hard blue eyes were as chilly as the ocean in April.

"Look Sam, just because you mark off the peanut butter jar to make sure no one's eating too much . . ."

They stopped short, glaring at each other, and then they slowly backed away. Sam went into the kitchen to stir the spaghetti sauce and Amanda followed and each determined to hold their arsenals in abeyance. They clung carefully to their manners through dinner, so conscious of cleansing each sentence of anything remotely dangerous that even the simplest of sentences sounded completely unnatural.

The evening continued, yellow and bruised and damaged, as they stood together washing and drying the dishes, careful not to break anything.

Amanda dried her hands while Sam attacked the bottom of a pot with violent determination. Finally, she could no longer bear the sound of Brillo on clean steel. "What is it, Sam?" she asked.

He continued scrubbing, harder and harder. He did

not want to look at her, not yet. "Nothing this city can cure," he said.

And when it was dark, when they were lying inside the dark and there was no place left to go, he said quietly, "I'm thinking of going home."

Amanda's muscles tightened. "For a visit?"

"I don't know."

"Oh."

There was no reason why he should have expected any stronger reaction than this, no reason at all, but . . . He turned away from her and yanked the sheets angrily into his grasp, there was no reason at all . . .

And he began to figure out exactly when he would leave, exactly how . . .

They gathered at Mrs. Easton's apartment, Sally and Frank and Amanda, for her sixtieth birthday. Sally had asked Amanda to bring Sam, but she had quickly declined. "Not now," she said.

They were going to take her out to a fancy dinner though she protested that wasn't what she wanted. "I'd rather just make dinner here," she said. But her daughters had insisted on taking her out and she did not have the energy to fight with them. Now they opened a bottle of champagne and gave her her gifts. A peach lace and silk nightgown to make her feel pretty, though they doubted she would ever wear it. A membership to the Metropolitan Museum of Art, though they doubted she would ever go. "How lovely," she said to both, and she smiled while Frank took a picture of her holding up the nightgown. "How lovely," she said again as she carefully folded it and put it back in its elegant box.

At dinner, Sally and Amanda struggled to keep the conversation light and topical as their mother's eyes wandered restlessly about the restaurant and Frank sat hunched up in the corner like a defeated question mark. Mrs. Easton smiled wanly as she pushed delicate slices of duck about her plate. "Yes I suppose I am too thin," she said when her daughters urged her to eat more. "I will have another glass of wine though. After all, it is my birthday.

"My," she continued distractedly, "sixty years old. It's rather hard to believe. It's not so bad though, not nearly as dreadful as thirty," she said. She looked directly at Amanda now for the first time all evening. "Thirty was most assuredly the worst. And I had a husband." She picked up her fork and again started pushing her food around. "Your father wrote me a delightful little poem that year," she said, smiling to herself.

Amanda said nothing. It certainly didn't seem the time to tell them she was going to visit him over the weekend.

Later, she dropped her mother off in a cab and watched as she walked slowly toward her building, stopping for a moment to talk to the doorman and then disappearing inside.

Downtown, the night was just beginning to fill and to vibrate, and Amanda told the driver to let her off ten blocks from her house. The shop windows were already becoming adorned with the festive boxes and bows of the holidays and she walked slowly, looking in each window as she went. Once, years ago, she had gotten a boy an expensive present and then been too embarrassed to give it to him. They hadn't really known each other all that well, after all. She wondered halfheartedly if Sam would be gone before Christmas, but she knew that he would. Just as well, she thought, one less present to buy.

As she walked by one of the vast new neon-striped restaurants, she saw Bill standing in the window, knocking on the glass and waving to her. She smiled and he motioned her in.

They kissed hello jauntily and as they squeezed out their own space at the bar, they fell immediately into the flirtatious banter that they both knew so well. Like any language that has not been used for a while, Amanda started out tentatively, gaining confidence as she went, until it was as if she had never left, never stopped the patter and pretense that used to make her glow in the dark. She warmed readily to it, to Bill, to the desire that was as pleasant a game as any. It was so easy, this swagger, like a mapped-out drawing of a dance step—you put one foot here, one foot there, it was so easy.

And yet, later, after they had played with each other for an hour and Bill put his arm around her and said, "Shall we go?" she surprised them both by answering that she would rather walk home alone. They kissed good night with a sadness that neither of them felt and Bill whispered in her ear, "Another night, then?" "You can bet on it," Amanda said.

Out on the street, she turned for a moment to look back inside the windows, and she saw Bill, leaning confidently up against another woman and talking animatedly. She smiled and started walking.

The floor of the train was awash with lakes of brown and gray slush and Amanda gave up trying to keep her feet dry. The dank chill was outside her and inside her too and as the train pulled out of the tunnel into the dingy morning she slid down into her seat and buried her face in her coat.

She felt distinctly empty-handed. She had no present for her father and his new bride, no house-warming gift, no wedding gift, nothing but a bunch of garishly dyed mums that she had picked up at the last minute in Grand Central Station. They were already tipped in brown.

Mr. Easton was waiting for her at the platform, waving frantically and calling out her name even before she had gotten off the train. Amanda's first impulse was to turn around, to get back on the train and continue to an unknown town with unknown people. At least she had cut the visit down to one night.

"Where's Joan?" Amanda asked as she got into her father's new BMW.

"She's back at the house, cooking up a storm. She can't wait to meet you."

They pulled up in front of a small, vaguely colonial two-bedroom house and entered through the back door into a bright blue and white kitchen. Joan, a ruffled apron covering her navy print dress, was basting a turkey. Not knowing quite what to do, Amanda held out her hand. "Nice to meet you," she said.

"We'll have none of that here," Joan said, and pulled her into a hug. Amanda could smell her hairspray as she looked over Joan's soft shoulder and watched her father nodding encouragement.

"Your father tells me you're in the fashion business," Joan said cheerfully as the two women set the table for dinner. "It must be so exciting."

"It's okay."

"Well you'll have to tell me all about it later. I hope we'll become very good friends. We could have lunch in the city sometime, do a little shopping. Maybe your sister could join us."

Amanda put the plates precariously close to the table's edge. "She's pretty busy with the baby these days."

"Of course. Well it will be just us two then."

They sat in the small dining room and drank club soda out of crystal goblets and wandered gingerly about, looking for something to discuss. Joan had never been married before and she reveled in the smallest of details, all of the "we's" that she finally had a right to. Her favorite expression seemed to be "Now, Edwin" and she said it with a single proprietary delight that seemed to delight Edwin too. Amanda had never wanted a drink so badly in her life.

"God grant me serenity," she muttered.

"What, dear?"

"Nothing."

It was an early evening.

When Amanda went down for breakfast the next morning, she came upon her father and his new wife embracing over the kitchen sink. Mr. Easton broke away as quickly as a red-handed teenager, but Joan pulled him right back. "We're newlyweds, after all," she said to Amanda conspiratorially. Amanda drank her coffee and stared glumly at the wallpaper, covered with a variety of birds perched atop their Latin names written in a fancy script. She decided to take an earlier train back.

"Well, darling," Mr. Easton said as he drove her to the station. "Isn't she wonderful?"

"Sure, Dad."

"I just knew you two gals would hit it off."

They sat in the car with little to say, waiting for the train. "How's your mother?" Mr. Easton asked finally.

"She's fine."

"Really? Is she really?"

"I said she was fine."

"Good. I'm glad. She has a birthday coming up, doesn't she?"

"You missed it."

"Oh."

"Look, Dad, you don't have to wait like this. Why don't you just let me out?"

"Don't be silly."

But Amanda insisted and her father left her standing hunched and shivering beneath the Plexiglas roof of the platform, waiting for her train home.

Sam's sublet was up on the first of December anyway. He sat down with a scotch-and-soda and continued his calculations. The loft, the jobs, everything, it seemed, was temporary. He could get out of it all. It was suddenly so clear, so easy. His pace quickened.

He had called his parents this afternoon to tell them the news, carefully wording it so that it would not sound like a surrender.

"Oh, sweetheart," his mother said. "That's wonderful. I just knew you'd come back. You just had to get it out of your system, that's all. Didn't I tell you that, Fred?" she asked her husband who was waiting his turn on the other extension.

"That's just what she said all right," he confirmed. "Now listen, Son, I'm sure you can get your old job back in a little while, and you can live with us until you get your feet back on the ground."

"Dad," Sam said, "I told you, I don't really know what I want to do."

"Well coming home is the first step," his mother interrupted. "This is where you belong. Besides, I'll bet Cathy can't wait to see you."

Their elation irritated Sam and he got off the phone as quickly as possible.

Among the papers on his desk was a letter from Cathy. He had only to skim it quickly to know what she would say. "Dear Sam, What a nice surprise to hear from you. Well, nothing's changed much since you've been gone. My class this year has some really bright kids in it and I like teaching more and more all the time . . ." Sam noted that she still dotted her *i*'s with big fat circles and skipped to the bottom of the page. ". . . My parents send their love. They miss you. Me too. Lots of love, Cathy." He folded up the letter and put it back in its envelope, remembering how he always knew exactly what Cathy would say, always knew exactly what she wanted, and it was like a warm bath, this knowing. Nothing else seemed quite as certain tonight as Cathy's predictability.

As he poured himself another drink, he noticed the clock and remembered that he was supposed to call Amanda. He shrugged and went back to the desk. It didn't much matter. She had become unreal to him, like a grainy Xerox of a photograph, a dotted caricature of the original. He knew that if he was hours late in calling her, if he didn't call her at all, he knew that she would barely so much as question him. It couldn't much matter then, he thought. When they made love now, he could feel her float away, wander away from their rhythm, away from him, only to rejoin him when it was too late. It was like fucking ashes. He took a large sip of his drink. He would call her when he was ready.

He pushed the figurings and the letters aside and took out some fresh paper. He had one last assignment to finish, one last piece on a minor celebrity he had interviewed the week before. She had lain on the couch in her hotel room, refusing to discuss her new album, preferring instead to compare notes on other minor celebrities, who was good in bed, who wasn't. Every now and then, she had interrupted her detailed appraisals to ask Sam, "Did you get that?"

He wrote the article quickly, thanking God with each sentence that it was to be the last of this kind. He wanted only to be done with it. This wasn't what he had meant, this wasn't what he had meant to do at all. He wanted to be done too with this city where everyone about him was getting ahead, getting going, getting, getting, getting . . .

He put the interview in a manila envelope and set it by the door. He thought about pouring himself another drink, he thought about being reckless and irresponsible and . . . But he went to the phone and dialed Amanda's number instead. He had promised to call her after all.

"What's this I hear about Sam's leaving?" Sally asked.

"He's going home for a while."

"For how long?"

"I don't know. A while."

"Is there another girl?"

"What makes you ask that?"

"Just a hunch."

"Well maybe you're right."

"I'd be careful of those small-town girls if I were you. They mean business. They know every Saturday night counts." Sally was just hitting her stride now. "They know how to get the job done. They know it's real life."

Amanda rolled her eyes. "You sound like a TV preacher warning me of Armageddon."

"Not Armageddon." Sally gave lip service to laughing. "Just good girls."

"Well there's nothing I could do about it anyway."

"Have you asked him to stay?"

Amanda was quiet for a minute. This had simply never occurred to her. She had accepted Sam's leaving as a *fait accompli*. And anyway, what right did she have to ask anything of him? "No," she said.

"You really are hopeless," Sally said. "Just what the hell are you waiting for? You think there's an endless supply of single men out there? I'd put up a fight if I were you."

Amanda laughed at this for the idea of fighting for a man, of competing or cajoling or manipulating, was as alien to her as honesty. She wouldn't have the slightest idea of how to go about it, even if she had wanted to. She could only watch him as he went.

"The only thing you haven't told me is that I'm not getting any younger," she said.

"Well you're not."

"Jesus, Sally, why don't you apply for a job as special adviser to Helen Gurley Brown?"

When she got off the phone with her sister, Amanda was hit suddenly with embarrassment and regret, for the act of showing any vulnerability or need, if only for advice, made her distinctly uncomfortable, and she moved rapidly about her apartment to get rid of its scent.

She dusted off her dresser and she turned on the television and she turned off the television and turned on the stereo and she darted about quickly and aimlessly, cigarette in hand, trying desperately to make up more amenable moods.

And what she came up with was this: She wanted Sam gone. If that was what he wanted, then good, fine, go. She wanted him gone. She put on a more raucous album and thought about all the good times she would have without him, the fine times, the fine men she would go out with. She thought about that feeling you can get with a new man, like diving into the ocean on a red-flag day. Good, fine, go, she thought.

And she thought too about how she used to love to go on the swings when she was little, how she liked that more than anything else, going up on those yellow swings, kicking the ground and going up, higher and higher, alone.

Their days became quiet, still, remote. They were decent and kind. They were waiting. They silently marked off each day. Now two weeks, now one . . . They withdrew into their manners, speaking in polite, conciliatory tones, each apprehensive of appearing too anxious. Only two weeks, only one . . .

Amanda watched as Sam packed up his books and his papers in cartons and shipped them home. She watched as he packed his clothes in a worn brown leather suitcase. She even offered to help.

On the night before Sam was to leave, they slept in their separate apartments. He had things to do, so many people to see, errands—she understood. In truth, he wanted to spend his last night in New York alone. He would go over to her place for breakfast before he left.

Sam spent a good part of the night wandering through the city's near-empty streets. Down Fifth Avenue with its brilliant jewels sleeping behind heavy gates and through the Village as the nightclubs spit out their tired dancers and back in his neighborhood, the enormous warehouses barren now—the city was like an ancient dowager to him, and he saw its layers and layers of rouge, its endless artifice, its silly vanities. And yet he could see too the flirtatious young girl underneath, the seductress, the siren he had first fallen for, and he knew that she would not be quite so easy to leave behind.

Amanda was breaking open eggs the next morning when the phone rang.

"I'm really sorry," Sam said, "but I didn't get as much done last night as I had hoped. All these last-minute loose ends. You know how it is. Anyway, it doesn't look like I'm going to be able to come over after all."

"Are you sure?"

"I'm sorry."

"Well good-bye then."

"Good-bye."

"Have a good trip."

"Thanks. You too."

"I'm not going anyplace."

"Right. Sorry. Good-bye."

Sam hung up and sat still. It was so easy. All he had to do was close his suitcase and leave. Maybe go to a diner near the bus station for some coffee. He bit his lip and bit it more. Suddenly, he grabbed his parka and bolted out the door.

Amanda was throwing food out when she opened the door and found Sam there, breathless. He touched her cheek lightly with his fingertips and looked at her for a long moment before he finally said, "Can I come in? I've only got a minute."

They sat at opposite ends of the couch, only partially facing each other, as awkward as if this were their first date. Sam turned toward her and started to speak and then slowly turned away. There was something, something he needed to know or to say or to ask or to hear before he left. Something. There had to be something.

"You know what our problem was?" he asked.

Amanda was stunned by the past tense, by its finality, it was like ice. "What?"

"We didn't talk enough. The mystery of what we created eventually overwhelmed the thing itself." Sam was floundering round and about, trying to find it, the thing itself. "We never seemed to really talk," he said without looking at her.

Amanda felt suddenly defensive, not of herself, but of them. It hadn't been all that bad. "Yes we did," she protested.

"No. Not really."

But if that was their problem then, it was their problem now too, and they continued to turn to and away from each other in little arabesques of eagerness and resignation. There seemed to be no words for this kind of good-bye, for neither of them knew what kind of good-bye it was.

They were running out of time. Sam reached suddenly to Amanda with brusque determination, pulling her by the back of her neck toward him. Perhaps he would find the sentence he was looking for inside of her. He kept his eyes open.

She let him fuck her. She lay still while he touched her and she did not touch him back. She lay still. She let him hump away. She did not know what to do or to say and so she lay still and did not make a sound. She wanted to make him feel as lonely as she did.

He dressed quickly, keeping his back to her. His fingers caught on his shirt buttons and he cursed angrily. Whatever it was he had had one last hope of reaching, he had come up empty-handed. He gave up on the buttons and put on his coat. He kissed her lightly on the forehead and walked to the door.

She stayed on the couch and watched him, and what

she was watching was this: the creases in his jeans at the back of his knees. The whitened creases that were his and only his. And these creases in his jeans that were his and only his moved her in a way nothing had and she suddenly realized that he was leaving and she wanted to run up and grab him and hold him tight. But she only sat still and watched him go.

Sam kicked a broken Thundertrain bottle halfway up the block and then he broke into a run, faster and faster, toward his suitcase, toward the station, toward home, where it was green and even and flat.

It was four in the afternoon when the bus let Sam off in front of the Allensville Elementary and Junior High School. He was the only passenger getting off there and the driver scowled and spit on the ground when he had to remove five suitcases before he found Sam's deep in the metal belly.

No one had come to meet him. Sam looked up and down the street at the few cars going quickly by and then he turned back to the low cement building. In one of the windows he could just make out a group of colorful paper snowflakes. From where he was standing he could see too the football team practicing across the road and he sat down on his suitcase and watched the defense going over and over its paces until the cold made him shiver and wince. It was time to go home.

It was only a five-minute walk down Sawmill Road to his parents' house and it felt as if his feet were fitting perfectly into prints he had left behind, like the crumbs of Hansel and Gretel, to help him find his way. The neighbors' porch lights were just beginning to flick on and the suitcase tugged firmly at his arm.

Sam hoped no one would be there. What he wanted most was this: to slip quietly inside and go upstairs, into his old bedroom and go to sleep. To wake up the next morning and go down to breakfast as if he had never been gone. To have his mother turn around and say, "More bacon, sweetie?"

As he climbed the front steps he noticed that there were new curtains in the living-room windows, a flowery beige lace, and there were no lights on. He had lucked out after all—they must be out Christmas shopping. He had placed the proper key in his back pocket a million light-years ago, back in New York, and now, finally, he took it out and opened the front door.

Lights flashed on and a huge chorus of "surprises" darted out at him. Over thirty people had gathered to welcome Sam back, his aunts and his uncles and his sisters and their husbands, his nieces and nephews and his college roommate and most of the staff of the Allensville *Weekly Ledger*. Sam stepped back and looked helplessly at the hungry swirl before him, his eyes finally resting on a homemade banner that hung crookedly across the room. It had "Welcome Home!!!" painted on it in bright blue tempora.

"Sweetheart." Mrs. Chapman came rushing at him, her massive arms reaching out before her. "Did you have a good trip?" "It was fine, Mom." Sam kissed her hello and moved on to his father. They shook hands stiffly and then Mr. Chapman patted him awkwardly on the back. "Good to see you, Son," he said.

In the living room, a table was set up with cold cuts and cakes and punch. Sam noted the 100-cup coffee urn that made the rounds of all the really important parties in the neighborhood and seemingly belonged to no one family. "So sin city was just too much for you, huh?" Ronnie, his college roommate, was grinning like a banshee. Sam smiled. "Well I'm glad you're back anyway, homeboy." "Glad to be back," Sam said. There were aunts and uncles then, there were lots of others. "Glad to be back," Sam kept saying, "glad to be back."

Out of the corner of his eye he saw Cathy standing quietly in the corner, her hands clasped in front of her, patiently waiting her turn. "Go on up and say hi to her," Mrs. Chapman said, nudging Sam in her direction. "She helped me put this whole thing together."

Sam started walking toward her. He had almost forgotten how pretty she was. She had cut her smooth auburn hair into a stylish chin-length bob and she was wearing a pale blue dress that showed off each of her curves. They kissed hello clumsily, aware that they were being watched. "I'm so glad you're back," she said softly. Sam nodded and fit his arm about her waist, fit it right into that familiar groove, and they headed back out into the room together.

Later, when he wandered into the kitchen to grab another beer, Sam came upon his mother standing barefoot in the corner, leaning pensively on the counter with her head not three inches from the clock radio. "Just wanted to check the score," she said impatiently, obviously not wanting to be distracted. "It's a big game for the Cavaliers. Third quarter. I'll be out in a minute. Is it a nice party, sweetie?"

Nancy waited for Amanda to say something. She walked about her on tiptoes, giving her extra berth, waiting for a look, a sigh, a sign, an opening. But none came.

Amanda bustled about the store in vast spasms of energy and cheerfulness—chatting up the customers she usually had no time for, wrapping the gifts they were busy selling with extra flourishes, bigger bows, eagerly opening the mail in search of interesting invitations, picking up the phone on the first ring. She had even come in early this morning. Nancy began to wonder if she could have been wrong after all, if it really hadn't wounded, hadn't cut. She watched Amanda carefully, looking for details.

Finally, before all of the sympathy that she was so eager to dispense went stale inside of her, she asked as lightly as she could, "So how did you and Sam leave things?"

Amanda shrugged. "I don't really know."

"What do you mean, you don't know? Didn't you talk about it?"

"We fucked about it."

"What does that mean?"

"Not a whole helluva lot." Amanda turned her back to Nancy and finished putting the skirts in size order, the sixes and the eights and the tens, the navies and the blacks. She didn't say anything else until she had gone in the back and gotten her things. "I'll see you tomorrow," she said, and she left Nancy to close up by herself.

Amanda walked slowly, absentmindedly kicking at clumps of snow with the pointed toes of her cowboy boots. She was glad he was gone. She was relieved. She was tired of that damned quizzical look on his face anyway. She was tired of trying to figure out what the question was. She was goddamned glad he was gone. And just to be sure, she began to recount all that was wrong between them.

And yet, despite her resolution, what she found herself going over, what she found herself counting and recounting, were all of the things that they had never done, all of the things they had never had. They had never had a real argument, they had never made up, they had never nursed each other through a cold, they had never celebrated anything together, they had never had their picture taken. In fact, Amanda realized that she had no picture of Sam, nor he of her, there had been no letters, no notes, no proof. She wrapped her scarf twice about her neck and pulled up the collar of her coat. The only thing that felt real to her was what was missing.

She picked up a tuna sandwich at the corner deli and she only nodded distractedly when Mr. Tomarillo said, "I hear we're due for more snow." She was no longer in the mood for talk, for pleasantries, for anything coming in or going out.

When she got home, Amanda poured herself a full glass of wine and turned on the news, spreading the sandwich out on its wax paper across her lap. She stared for a long while at the images of Central America alternating with close-ups of Dan Rather's face, back and forth, back and forth, before she realized that she was utterly unable to follow the report. She strained forward and tried to pay closer attention, but it was as if Dan were speaking a foreign language. No matter what she did, fiddling with dials and antennas and positions, she could not understand a word of it. It was just babbling—ceaseless, senseless, taunting. An injection of panic shot through Amanda's veins.

She left the uneaten sandwich on the bed and went frantically into the living room and picked up the phone.

"Bill," she said, trying to slow her voice to hide the eagerness, "how about coming over for dinner?"

But the need had punched its way through her steady tone and knocked Bill off guard. "Dinner would be too heavy," he said brightly. "How about hors d'oeuvres?"

Amanda accepted the terms and laughed halfheartedly. "Whatever," she said.

Sally was gaining weight. With great gusto and determination and the energy that revenge can bring, Sally was gaining weight. She sat across from Frank and helped herself to another piece of garlic bread, cocking her head slightly and registering his scowl. In the morning, he would greet her with a new exercise regimen, a new nutritional report clipped and underlined. Or perhaps he would come home from work with some metal contraption guaranteed to tone her tummy, firm her upper arms, keep her breasts from sagging.

"How are you doing with your Christmas shopping?" she asked Amanda cheerfully as the waiter brought a second bottle of the nouveau Beaujolais.

"Actually, I haven't even started yet."

"Why don't you hire Frank?" Sally asked as she poured them both more wine. Frank had his hand over his glass. "It's a little late for him, he likes to have his lists and alternatives compiled by early November, but since you're a member of the family . . ."

Frank clearly did not like the tone in his wife's voice. In fact, he did not like the increasing frequency of these little family dinners at all.

Amanda smiled faintly. She was not in the mood for

a scene tonight. Not that there would be a real scene, it never quite reached that point, but she was in no mood to be the mirror they shadow-boxed in front of. Not tonight.

"What did you get Mom?" she asked.

Sally took a large gulp of wine. "In duplicate," she said.

Amanda did not follow. "What?"

"He types the lists in duplicate."

Frank sat back and crossed his arms while Amanda looked over to see if Sally was kidding. He stared back at her coldly. "Well it makes perfect sense," he said. "That way we can each have a copy handy when we go shopping." He turned his eyes to Sally now. "I do wish you'd remember to cross an item off of both lists though. You're making things unnecessarily confusing."

Sally shrugged at him and smiled at Amanda. "See?"

The music had suddenly gotten noticeably louder, filling the already noisy restaurant with the quirks and quavers of an atonal rock opera. It was the restaurant of the week though and the lucky diners merely raised their voices, glad to be there.

"If I wanted to go to a damned nightclub, I would have gone to a damned nightclub," Frank said. "Who chose this place anyway?"

Sally ignored him. "Any word from Sam?"

Amanda fiddled with her silverware. "He's only been gone a few days, Sally." She put the knife into the fork's tongs over and over again. "Besides, we didn't promise to write or anything."

Sally looked up at her sister. "But . . ."

"Drop it," Amanda said. There was a disgruntled pause. "By the way, I went to see Dad."

"You what?"

"I went to see Dad and his new wife."

"I don't believe it. I just don't believe it. You went to see him and you didn't even tell me you were going? Why didn't he ask me to come? Did he even ask about me? I don't believe it, I just don't believe it."

"Would you have come?"

"Of course not. Well maybe. I don't know. Jesus. What was she like?"

"I'll tell you one thing, she keeps him in line."

"What does that mean?"

"Well . . ."

Sally leaned even farther forward and it was as if Frank had disappeared from the table. Which would have suited all three of them. "What does she look like? Is he drinking? Did you tell Mom? Oh God, you didn't tell Mom, did you?"

"Calm down, Sally. One thing at a time."

"I don't believe it." Sally paused for a second to order the pecan pie. "I just don't believe it."

Sam woke up later than usual and went downstairs to have a cup of coffee. His father had already left for work and his mother was in the living room watching the last minutes of the *Today* show. Sam had forgotten about the constant hum and glow of the television at home, forgotten that women all across town had already gotten a good two hours of viewing in. Later they would analyze Bryant Gumbel's performance in minute detail and speculate once again on what kind of mother Jane Pauley was. Mrs. Chapman always took their advice seriously too. Once, when they had done a three-part series on models' tips for the average woman, she had appeared at dinner each night with a different part of her face outlined and emphasized. When she painted her toenails a glossy dark scarlet, Mr. Chapman finally turned to her and said, "I prefer a more natural look, Pat." The polish remained though, until it slowly wore away and all that was left were tiny specks of scarlet on her broad and yellowed nails.

"Do you want me to fix you something?" she asked now, without taking her eyes from the set. Bryant was standing next to the president of Hammacher Schlemmer, holding up one extraordinary gift suggestion after another.

"No thanks, Mom. I'll get it myself."

He went into the kitchen and poured himself a cup of tepid coffee that had been brewed hours ago and got out a box of some new fiber-filled cereal. His mother continued to buy everything in the huge family sizes despite the fact that there was no family at home and the cereal didn't taste quite fresh.

After breakfast Sam wandered aimlessly about the house for a while, picking up this or that, lingering, bored, aware that his mother's eyes were fixed on him, as if she feared that by loosening her watch for a moment he might slip away again. She had been following him about like this since he got back, just a few paces behind, waiting for him to make a move, waiting for him to store his suitcase, waiting for him to announce his intentions.

Sam showered and dressed and walked into town. Bell-shaped ornaments hung from the lamps and there was silver tinsel every place he looked. Not having any plans, he decided that he might as well do some Christmas shopping and he headed optimistically in the direction of the bigger of Allensville's two drugstores. Sam found himself wandering up and down the cluttered aisles, staring at the bottles and puffs and miniature shell-shaped soaps, forgetting whom he had to buy presents for, forgetting whom he knew. After a few more futile trips back and forth, he went to the register and picked up a postcard of the old courthouse and a copy of the *Ledger* and headed for the Blue Bird Diner.

The wife of the school-board president had been in a minor car accident out by the mall and the utility company was asking for another increase in rates and the high school had lost again. Sam glanced at the recipe of the week and folded up the paper and got out the postcard.

He didn't know what to say. Nothing. He had nothing to say. It took him fifteen minutes to write, "Dear Amanda,

I made it here in one piece." He ordered another cup of coffee and added, "It's strange here." He had nothing else to say, no other sentences came. He signed it "Yours, Sam."

At the post office, Rita Carlson gave him a huge smile when he got to her window. "Well I'll be," she said. "I heard rumors about you coming back. But I said no. I said you were gone for good." Sam smiled politely and handed her the postcard, knowing that she would read it as soon as his back was turned.

On his way home, Sam decided to stop into the *Ledger*'s offices. Just to say hello.

Sam took Cathy to the movies. They sat in the back row and Cathy rested her hand gently on Sam's thigh. Halfway through the picture, he put his arm around her and pulled her close and it felt good. It felt good and clear to be at the movies with a girl, a girl you knew wanted you, your girl, on a Friday night. There was nothing wrong with that.

Afterward, they went to The Tavern for a drink and ran into Cathy's older brother, John. The three of them sat at the end of the bar while Springsteen poured out of the jukebox, one hit after another, and the bartender closed his eyes and wailed along. "Glory days, they'll pass you by, glory days . . ."

"I'll bet nightlife in the Big Apple beat the hell out of this," John said.

Cathy glared over at him. The last thing she wanted to hear about was the benefits of living in New York. It was as if she thought she could erase the past year and a half by simply ignoring it. It was a lapse. A temporary fling. Boys will be boys. All that really mattered was that he was home now. Where he belonged. "Did you hear about the new tennis courts they're building out at the high school?" she asked.

Sam nodded.

"Is the housing shortage really as bad as they say?" John went on.

"I guess so," Sam said. "Though I had a pretty good deal."

Cathy just sat there and didn't ask any more questions. The two men continued to work around her silence and Sam noted the slightest hint of jealousy in John's voice, but in the end, he stood up and slapped Sam on the back. "Well hell," he said. "You're pushing thirty anyway. Time to stop playing around." He winked theatrically at Cathy and then he left the two of them alone.

Cathy was suddenly as shy and demure as a choir girl and it rubbed Sam wrong. After all, the first time they had slept together was over seven years ago. After another drink though, she looked up at him from her lowered eyelids and she said, "Do you want to go back to my place?" and Sam said "yes." Cathy chattered nervously about a deaf girl in her kindergarten class as they drove back to the garage apartment she rented from her parents.

He remembered the smell of the herbal shampoo she used, he remembered the way her breasts filled his hands and the curve of her hips and this too was good and almost clear. "I've missed you," she whispered in his ear and she insinuated herself around and above and below him, moving and moaning in ways she never had before. She seemed so anxious to please him that Sam wondered if she had been reading books on the matter. He thought for an instant about his last act of necrophilia with Amanda and then he didn't think about it at all. "You make me weak in the knees," Cathy said afterward. Sam almost laughed but he couldn't—she said it with such sincerity.

She shook him gently awake just as the sky was slipping into its first dove-gray light. "Darling, darling," she whispered with velvet-covered insistence. Sam opened his eyes slowly, not wanting to show that he hadn't the vaguest idea where he was. "Darling, wake up. I think you'd better go."

Sam stared at Cathy in utter bewilderment.

"It's just that, well you know, it's not that my parents interfere or anything. And you know how they feel about you. But I'd rather they didn't see you leave in the morning."

Sam groaned but he did not protest. He got out of bed without saying anything and pulled on his jeans. Cathy walked him to the door. "Will I see you later?" she asked.

"Sure," he said and he kissed her good-bye and walked down the creaking steps and out onto the street and past her parents' windows, where all the lights were dark.

"You look like an old Spanish lady in mourning," Bill said when he came in. Amanda was wearing a long black skirt, a black turtleneck, and a black sweater. She was carrying a box of tissues.

She laughed. "Just a cold."

Bill helped himself to some brandy and followed her inside to where the television was already on. He settled in comfortably, kicking off his shoes and plumping pillows. They had been doing this for a long time, after all, this slow late-night tango of theirs where boredom and desire dipped and swooned, they had been doing it for years.

"You don't taste sick," Bill said when he finally pulled Amanda down to kiss her.

Amanda coughed a little in response.

Bill smiled. "I'll fuck the cold out of you," he said.

Amanda rolled her eyes. "The male ego knows no bounds."

They fooled around somewhat aimlessly for a while and eventually Amanda got up to go to the bathroom, wearing only Bill's Shetland sweater.

She washed her face slowly and then wiped off the charcoal makeup that had settled like an etching of a leaf into the new puzzlement of lines beneath her eyes. She brushed her hair back, took another look at her clean face in the mirror and went back to the bedroom.

As she climbed in beside Bill and began to fit herself into his arms, Amanda was hit by the oddest sensation. She jumped warily back, unable to place it. It took her a moment to realize that what she had been hit with was the strongest whiff of herself.

Bill smiled impishly. "I put on some of your perfume while I was waiting for you."

Amanda tried again to get close to him but it was too jarring, too odd. She sat up abruptly and turned on the lights.

"Are you tired?" she asked.

Bill looked up at her hopefully. "Nope."

"Good. Come with me," she said and led him into the bathroom.

He sat on the toilet with his face raised to her like a child's, full of trust and expectation, while she carefully washed over it with the lotions and powders that she used on herself each morning. The colors were just right for him, for in fact Bill and Amanda had almost exactly the same coloring, the same leanness and fine bones and light brown hair. It was one of the things about them—this similarity of appearance. His eyes fluttered nervously at the approach of the pencils and wands, but her touch was gentle and sure and it did not take long. When she was done, she dipped her brush in water and slicked back his hair.

"Let's see what we have here," Bill said as he stood up, impatient to see her portrait.

And they stood side by side in the mirror, she with her clean face and his sweater, he with her coral lips and smoky eyes, looking at themselves, at the other, at themselves.

It was past two by now and they were both suddenly worn out and they went back to bed and neither felt much like making love.

In the morning, Amanda pulled Sam's postcard out of her purse once again while Bill took a shower. She was still staring at it, the shape of the letters, the blue sky above the courthouse, when Bill came out and started to moonwalk naked across the living room.

"What a talented fellow," she said. "But don't you have a job to go to?"

There were other men. There were always other men when you didn't care. In fact, Amanda had long suspected that this was her secret with men, this not caring that could be slipped on with such casual defiance, like a broken-in leather jacket. And so now especially, there were other men, besides Sam, besides Bill, there were other men, there were a thousand ways not to spend the night alone.

After work, she went with Nancy to a gallery opening in the East Village. Crowds of people were gathered out on the street despite the cold, clutching little plastic cups of German white wine. Everyone, men and women, seemed to be wearing enormous overcoats in shades of gray and black and it was such a tiny gallery that they had to take turns going inside to look at the work. The name of the show was "Mythical Beasts and Bores"—photographs of downtown celebrities.

Amanda and Nancy side-stepped their way in and like everyone else, they looked first at the faces in the crowd, looked for friends, business acquaintances, lovers, contacts . . .

"There's no one here," Amanda said immediately.

"It's your open mind I love," Nancy said. "Try circulating."

The light was the extraordinary harsh white of an examining room and like most light, it made Amanda want to hide. She stayed close to Nancy and let her do most of the talking and the laughing, content to be her shadow, nodding when she had to, smiling noncommittally. The artists stood by their pictures in gray and black overcoats and tried to look blasé and most succeeded remarkably well. Amanda made her way through to the back room where they kept the price list and the wine.

In a few minutes Jack arrived and being one of the few people who had actually come to see the work, he wanted to leave immediately. Promising the gallery owner that he would come back when it was less crowded, he gave Nancy a look and she gave Amanda a look and the three of them went around the corner to have a drink.

The bar was full of refugees from the show and it took them fifteen minutes to get seats. The bartender was busy showing slides of his work to a well-dressed lady at the service station and it took them another fifteen minutes to order their drinks—a beer for Jack, a screwdriver for Amanda, club soda with lime for Nancy.

"Are you on some sort of a health kick?" Amanda asked skeptically.

Jack looked at her incredulously. "You mean she didn't tell you?"

"Tell me what?"

"We're pregnant," he said proudly and he put his arm on the back of Nancy's chair.

Amanda looked at Nancy for confirmation. "Why didn't you tell me?"

"I've been trying to all day, but you didn't seem to be in the best of moods."

"So what?"

Nancy laughed. "To tell you the truth, I'm scared of

you on days like that." She smiled gently now. "I'm sorry. I should have told you."

Amanda paused and put it away and then she kissed Nancy and she kissed Jack. "I'm so happy for you," she said. "Congratulations." And then there was an unusual silence as the pregnancy pulled up a seat at the bar.

On their way out, Nancy and Jack asked Amanda over for dinner, but she said she was too tired. She kissed them both again and told them again how happy she was, and she really was. And then she walked home alone, past other gallery openings, past other clusters of people in their gray and black overcoats, clutching their plastic cups of wine.

It had become a city of wind-up dolls, scurrying madly about, speeded up, bumping into each other, bumping into walls, backing up, scurrying on, expressionless. All about her, it seemed that there were people younger, faster, busier . . .

Amanda stood on the main floor of Bloomingdale's in the dizzy maze of black and white and makeup and mirrors. Her eyes wandered desperately about trying to find something to rest on, something to fix and to steady her, something that would make sense. She was conscious that standing still was not quite acceptable behavior and people knocked into her and scowled as they brushed past. Suddenly, her eyes focused on an enormous perfume bottle in front of her, coming closer and closer and closer. Behind it, a man in a black and yellow tuxedo was smiling professionally at her. "Try some Giorgio, ma'am?" he asked. The bottle was huge, menacing, and Amanda clutched instinctively at her hair and pleaded, "No. No, please don't . . ."

"Okay, honey," the gentleman said, backing up. "Calm down. Jeez, I thought I was uptight."

"I'm sorry," Amanda said. She was shaking still. "I just really don't like that perfume."

"I can see that," he said, and headed toward a woman in a sable coat. "Try some Giorgio, ma'am?"

Amanda left the store by the side entrance on 59th Street and went into a discount drugstore to buy some Excedrin. Then she went into the take-out coffee shop next door and asked for a glass of water. The elderly Greek man behind the counter watched as she struggled to open the little tin case and take out two tablets. She looked up apologetically. "Christmas shopping. You know."

He smiled paternally. "I bet you didn't have any breakfast. You can't go shopping without a good breakfast in you. Why don't you let me fix you something?"

Amanda said she was late for an appointment and she walked out into the street. She looked for a moment at the shoppers rushing in and out of the fat white building and knew she really ought to try again. But she took a taxi home instead.

She wanted to write Sam back. She had been wanting to write Sam back for days. The problem was she didn't know what to say. She sat on the floor of her living room and stared at the stationery in front of her. Dear Sam, It's strange here too. Yours, Amanda. No. Not that.

Dear Sam, What the hell are you doing in Bumfuck, Ohio, anyway? Yours, Amanda. No. Not that either.

Yours, Sam. What the fuck did that mean—Yours, Sam?

Dear Sam, I'm smoking two packs of cigarettes a day and fucking all the wrong people and pleasure never seems to feel like pleasure. Yours, Amanda. She crumpled up the blank sheet of paper and threw it against the wall.

Finally, Amanda wrote Sam about what New York looked like, about the giant snowflake that hung mid-air above Fifth Avenue and the skating rink made of diamonds in Tiffany's windows and about the hustlers on St. Mark's

Place who spread their wares so deep that you had to walk out in the street. She wrote him that Sally hadn't found a job and Legacies had been written up in the *Times* and Nancy was pregnant and she had seen their phone-beating bum uptown dressed as a Salvation Army Santa Claus. And then she wrote that she missed him and she signed it "With love," and she grabbed her coat and ran out to mail it before she changed her mind. She needed a fresh pack of cigarettes anyway.

It was as if she had a calendar hidden in some closet with the proper sequence of events written in, the proper order and progression. He could see her going home each night and smiling to herself as she crossed off now one thing, now the next. He wouldn't be surprised if there were a diamond solitaire someplace that she was paying off in weekly installments. And all he had to do was close his eyes and slide.

Sam and Cathy agreed to visit with both of their families on Christmas Eve and they went to the Chapmans' first. They sat in the living room and drank eggnog, smiling at each other and eyeing the presents under the tree. Sam's mother hovered anxiously about, noting with pleasure that they were holding hands, offering them more to eat, more bits of gossip, more reasons to stay.

"Did you go to the *Ledger* the other day?" Mr. Chapman asked.

"Yes, Dad."

"And?"

"And they said they might have some assignments for me. Nothing full time."

Mrs. Chapman could not contain herself. "Oh, sweetie, that's wonderful. You'll be back where you were in no time."

Sam crossed and uncrossed his legs. "I'm just doing it because I need the money. It's nothing permanent."

Cathy bit her lower lip and did not say anything.

Mrs. Chapman decided it would be best to ignore this last bit. "Did you hear that, Fred?" she said. "I told you, it just takes kids a little longer these days, that's all."

"In my day, thirty wasn't a kid. I had a family at his age."

Sam had heard all this before of course and he did not feel like hearing it now. He stood up brusquely, pulling Cathy with him, and said they had to get going. Outside, he dropped her hand and walked angrily ahead of her, kicking at imaginary obstacles on the ground. He got in the car and slammed the door and as he backed quickly out of the driveway, Cathy put her hand on his and said soothingly, "They didn't mean anything by it."

"Of course not," Sam said and pulled his hand away. "Let's go get your family over with."

Later, after they had had more eggnog and more food and the same gossip, they finally made their way out of her parents' dining room and up the icy steps to the garage apartment.

Sam sank into the couch with a loud sigh of relief and kicked off his boots and flicked on the television. Cathy was standing by the small refrigerator and in a moment she came over with a bottle of champagne and turned off the television and sat down next to Sam. She had a serious look on her face.

"Are you staying?" she asked as she removed the wire from the cork.

"I just got here."

"I mean here. Allensville. Are you staying?"

Sam groaned and sat up straighter. "For a while."

"What does that mean?"

"Look, Cathy, it's been a long night. Can't we talk about this some other time?"

Cathy shook her head. "No," she said. "I need to know what your plans are."

Sam stood up angrily. "I thought you had that all figured out."

Cathy put the bottle down and started to cry softly. Sam watched her for a couple of minutes without moving and then he went back and sat next to her and took her in his arms. "I'm sorry," he said.

Then they opened the champagne and they toasted the season and Sam turned the television back on.

Sally stood in Amanda's living room with her coat still on, flushed and breathless with excitement. "I've made up my mind," she said.

Amanda was still getting dressed, and she stood in front of the full-length mirror with her pants at her knees, examining her hips. "About what?" she yelled in distractedly.

"About Frank, about my life."

Satisfied for the moment with her figure, Amanda pulled up her pants and went inside. "What are you talking about?"

"I'm leaving him."

"You're what?"

"I'm leaving Frank."

"Christ, Sally, when did you decide this?"

"I've been thinking about it for a while. But you've got to promise me not to say anything. I told him I was just coming over to help you carry stuff. You've got to act completely normal tonight."

"When are you going to tell Mom?"

"As soon as I tell Frank."

Amanda looked at Sally and laughed. "You haven't mentioned to your husband that you're leaving him?"

Sally shrugged. "I will."

"When?"

"As soon as the time is right."

When Amanda and Sally arrived at Mrs. Easton's, Frank was already there with Maggie. There were season's greetings and controlled kisses and only Maggie seemed excited as she ran up to her mother, her thick white tights falling in rolls about her chubby thighs. In the corner there was a small tree that looked like it had been pulled out of a closet for many years of Christmases, despite the fact that it was real, and Sally and Amanda added their presents to the collection underneath its faded branches.

Amanda poured everyone a sherry, giving Frank just a little bit more—knowing he was on his way out, she was feeling just a bit more kindly toward him—and Mrs. Easton began to distribute the gifts.

Glossy boxes from Bendel's and Saks piled up at Sally's and Amanda's feet and they took turns opening them and exclaiming. Mrs. Easton watched with anticipation and surprise as each of the gifts was opened, as if she had forgotten what she had bought. At times, the surprise turned to consternation as a particularly odd article was pulled from its box. "Oh my," she said as Amanda peeled away some tissue paper and uncovered a lacy black bra for a full-figured woman. "Oh my. That's not what I meant at all. It's not like Bendel's to send the wrong thing." And Mrs. Easton explained that she had done all of her Christmas shopping by phone and she would be happy to phone again and have everything taken away. "This really isn't what I meant at all," she said again and she went into the kitchen to see to dinner.

Frank pulled a small blue box out of his pocket and handed it to Sally. "Here," he said. "Why don't you open this?"

"I thought we were going to wait until tomorrow,"

Sally said as she looked at the box and tugged at the end of her skirt.

"I'd like you to open this now."

Sally took the box and opened it slowly and found a gold necklace with a heart-shaped pendant made of diamonds. She stared at it for a moment and then looked shyly up at her husband. "It's beautiful," she said. Amanda watched as Frank put it on for her. He kissed her on the back of her neck and then he went into the kitchen to see if he could be useful.

Still smiling shyly, Sally looked down at Maggie, who was busy putting the colorful ribbons into her mouth and drooling colorful drool. Sally picked her up and wiped her chin and tried to kiss her, but Maggie wanted only to swallow the shimmering heart.

Like an amputated limb, he could still feel its absent pulse, he could still make out the ghost of its outline. It was a shadow in the night, there and yet not there, haunting. That's how he missed the city.

Sam sat at his desk looking out of the *Ledger*'s main-floor windows. The few people who passed by walked with their heads bent against the wind, their puffy down-covered arms of orange and green wrapped tightly about their torsos for protection. It suddenly irritated Sam how large and clumsy they all looked, and how they did not seem to care. He turned his eyes back to his desk.

His first assignment was a lengthy piece on a twenty-six-year-old man who had kidnapped a twelve-year-old girl. He said it was love. His attorney said it was insanity. Or rather, diminished capacity. The inability to distinguish right from wrong. It had happened only a couple of towns away. Everyone knew someone who knew someone who was sure to be involved. Everyone had something to say. "Your kind of story," the editor had said when he handed Sam the basic information. Sam read other cases of diminished capacity and took notes, wondering what the editor meant.

At six o'clock, Cathy came to pick him up and they

left their cars parked out back. The apartment she wanted to show him was only three blocks away. It was lucky she knew about it, it was lucky her friend was getting married, it would be perfect, absolutely perfect, he'd see. Sam knew he couldn't continue to live in his parents' house and he figured he might as well have a look.

They picked up the keys in Riley's Liquor Store and Mrs. Riley took them upstairs to show them around. Sam said little as Mrs. Riley pointed out all of the fine points to Cathy, the exposure on three sides and the modern bathroom and the proximity to the Safeway. He walked a few paces behind the women, looking at nothing in particular, nodding when it seemed called for. Finally, Mrs. Riley turned to him and smiled. "Well, I'll leave you two young people alone for a while," she said. "The lease will be downstairs in the store."

Cathy sat in the window seat and looked at Sam, leaning against the wall and absentmindedly chipping off paint with his thumbnail. "Well, what do you think?" she asked.

"It's okay."

Cathy stood up. "You're not going to do better than this, Sam," she said. "The rent's low and it's close to work. All it needs is a little paint."

Sam continued chipping away for a minute and then he went in to have another look at the bedroom. He stood looking out the window for a while as the traffic light turned to red and to green and back to red. He wondered if Amanda had made up the part about seeing their bum dressed as a Salvation Army Santa, he wondered if he rang the bell in the same rhythm he beat the phone.

"Well?" Cathy said when he came back out. "Well?"

"I just don't know," Sam said impatiently.

"You're not going to do better than this," Cathy said

angrily. "You'll see. You're not." It sounded like a threat.

Sam went down to the liquor store and told Mrs. Riley that he'd appreciate some time to think it over.

"How long?" she asked.

Sam didn't know how long.

"I'll tell you what," Mrs. Riley said. "I'll hold the lease for you for one week. How does that sound?"

Sam said that sounded more than fair and he thanked her and he and Cathy left the liquor store and headed toward their cars.

She sat with the Sunday paper sprawled before her, inky and unread. It was late in the morning, but Amanda still hadn't brushed her teeth or washed her face and she probably wouldn't for hours. She started when the phone rang and the coffee she had been holding jumped over the sides of the mug and into her lap.

"Hello?"

"Hello? Amanda? This is Mrs. Easton."

It didn't sound anything like her mother. "Who?"

"Mrs. Easton. Joan. Your stepmother."

"Oh. Right. Yes?"

"I hate to ask you this. I'm sure it's nothing. Nothing at all, but . . ."

"Yes?"

"Yes. Well now it's nothing to worry about . . . But. Well. Have you by any chance seen your father?"

"My father? Why would I have seen my father?"

"Well, it's just that . . . Well, he seems to have disappeared."

Amanda's first impulse was to laugh. It was a laugh she had perfected a long time ago to cover the sound of her stomach sinking twenty feet. But Joan was new to this, she hadn't had time to learn it yet. Amanda yanked her hair back and asked, "How long has he been gone?"

"Oh not long, not long at all. Since noon yesterday. It's just that, well, he missed his meeting last night and . . ."

"Well, I haven't heard from him," Amanda said.

"What about your sister?"

"I haven't heard from her either."

Joan cleared her throat.

"Sorry," Amanda said. "It's just that . . . Look, he'll turn up when he's good and ready. But if you want, I'll call around."

"Oh, yes, would you?"

"Sure. Joan?"

"Yes?"

"Did you check the hospitals?"

"Yes."

Amanda hung up the phone and looked around for her cigarettes. The only pack she could find was empty and she picked up the pillows from the couch and threw them on the floor and got a splinter as she peered under the bed and finally she went to the garbage and found a butt covered with coffee grounds. She wiped it off and lit it. "Shit," she said out loud. She sat by the phone, lighting and relighting the filthy cigarette end. "Shit, shit, shit."

Sally was of course vividly awake and clearing away her family's breakfast dishes. "What are you doing up so early?" she asked Amanda lightly.

"Joan called."

"Who?"

"Dad's wife."

"You two are getting awfully chummy."

"Look, Sally, it seems Dad is on the missing list."

Amanda heard some silverware clanking into the sink.

"Oh, God," Sally said. "Well what are we supposed to do about it?"

"I don't know. But she's really worried. He's been sober since he met her."

"And now it's time to wake up and smell the whiskey."

"Goddammit, Sally."

"Okay, okay, sorry." She took a deep breath and tried to control her voice. "I just don't see what we can do. We never could do anything. She checked the hospitals, didn't she?"

"Yes."

"Well I'm sure he'll come back. Whatever you do, don't call Mom, okay?"

"Okay."

By midafternoon, Amanda could no longer just sit there. She hadn't been able to go out for cigarettes for fear that if her father called he wouldn't leave a message, and if it was Joan, well she hadn't been able to go out, she hadn't been able to do anything, and anyway, she had a feeling, just a feeling . . .

"Mom," she said. "I don't want you to get excited. I know this is a crazy question. But have you heard from Dad?"

"Why yes. He's right here."

"He's what?"

"He's right here. I was just making us some tea. Would you like to talk to him?"

Amanda breathed deeply. "No."

She called Sally and told her of their father's whereabouts.

"Jesus fucking Christ," Sally said.

There was a long pause.

"Well," Amanda said. "I suppose I'd better call Joan."

Amanda was beginning to distrust the night. Often she found herself lying in the dark for hours, listing all of the things that could decay, all of the things that could fly apart, could rot . . .

On New Year's Eve, she decided to paint her apartment. White. Clean, new, white. With manic energy, she rushed about, emptying the shelves and binding the records and removing the paintings and shoving the furniture into the middle of the two rooms. She was certain that it would help.

She enjoyed the labor, the sound of the wet paint rolling onto the walls, covering the dirt and the scars. Even the acrid smell and the soreness in her shoulders were good. She stopped for just a minute to listen to the bells and the hoots at midnight and then she continued with her work, dipping, stretching, rolling.

It was past two when she finally finished the living room and she peeled off her splattered sticky clothes and went naked into the kitchen to get a glass of wine. She lay down on the mattress in the middle of the room and drank slowly and it was clean and still and quiet. When the phone rang, it took her seven rings to find it.

"Hello?"

"Amanda? I was just about to hang up."

"Sam? Where are you?"

"In a bar. I just wanted to wish you a Happy New Year. How are you?"

"Fine, fine."

There was an echo, an echo so pervasive that everything Amanda said came back to her three seconds later, sitting atop Sam's words in a mangle of their two voices. She asked if it was the same on his end, but he said no, on his end everything was fine. Nevertheless, she got his number and called him back. But the echo was still there.

The only way around it was for Sam to do all of the talking, it was the only thing that Amanda could understand, and besides, his voice was so good to her, she just wanted to listen to it all night long. Sam soon grew impatient though.

"I want to hear about you," he protested.

"There's nothing to tell," she said. "I'm in the middle of the room."

"You're what?"

"Nothing. Tell me more about you. What have you been doing?"

"Not much. I've started to do some work for the *Ledger* again."

Everything inside fell a little. "Oh. That's nice."

Sam laughed. "Well I wouldn't go that far."

They talked for a few more minutes and finally Sam said, "We should get off. This is getting awfully expensive."

"But it's on my bill," Amanda protested.

"Still . . ."

"Well . . ."

"Well . . ."

"Good night then," she said.

"Good night," he said.

And then she added softly, "I really do miss you," and like everything else, it reverberated in her ear so that she could not tell if he had said, "I really do miss you," too or if it was just the sound of her own voice coming back to her.

Sam put the phone back in its cradle and leaned his forehead up against the cold black box for a minute or two, and then he went back out into the boisterous bar, where Cathy was waiting impatiently for him.

And Amanda went and got herself another glass of wine and put on a low country moan of an album and she lay back and watched the soft dappled neon light come in through the blinds and stick to the wet walls.

"Hoods."

"Hoods?"

"Hoods," Nancy said emphatically, impatiently. "How do you feel about hoods?"

"Fine, I guess."

"Another definite opinion. Really, Amanda, do you think we should go with hoods on the new sweaters?"

Amanda shrugged and continued to examine the first of the spring clothes that had just begun to come in, as tempting and luscious as out-of-season fruit. "If you think so," she said.

"I'm asking your opinion."

"I didn't realize hoods were such a burning issue."

"That's not the point," Nancy said.

"What is the point?"

"The point is that you never give me a straight answer about anything."

Amanda had walked over to where Nancy was standing and as Nancy stared at her in growing frustration, Amanda stared at the brass and rhinestone earrings in the glass case she was leaning on.

"What are you talking about, Nancy?"

"I guess what I'm talking about is this partnership thing. I've been asking you about it for at least six months and I still have no idea what your plans are."

Amanda looked up at her for an instant and then she looked away. "I know," she said softly.

"Well?"

"I don't know."

Nancy rubbed her rounded stomach unconsciously and her voice went up an octave. "Well I need to know," she said. "I need to know what your intentions are."

"You want me to make an honest woman out of you?"

"Jesus, will you just stop it, Amanda? I'm in no mood for your cool act."

Amanda looked at Nancy, startled—it was like a bad fall, going over and over, in slow motion, time outside of time. She remained silent.

Nancy waited for a moment and then she spoke again in a lower, a softer voice. "I'm sorry," she said. "I didn't mean that. I've been a little moody these days. But I really do need to know what you're planning on doing. I would love to have you as my partner and I think you'd be great at it, but I just can't wait around endlessly for you to make up your mind. I think you owe me an answer."

"Owe you?"

"Yes, owe me. How about one week?"

"That's it? Just one week?"

"This isn't exactly a new idea, Amanda. Besides, maybe it would be good for both of us to have some sort of a deadline."

"Don't tell me what's good for me," Amanda sputtered as she stormed past Nancy to get her coat.

"Please, Amanda, don't leave like this. Let's sit down and talk. Please."

Amanda ignored her.

On her way out the door, she turned around for just a second and hissed, "I fucking hate hoods."

On stage, the performers were playing "The Dating Game." Amanda stood next to Bill in the small crowded room and watched the proceedings. The emcee was wearing an oversized double-knit suit and there were three bachelors sitting on rickety stools facing the audience. They all looked vaguely familiar, though they were wearing so much makeup it was hard to tell. The audience was yelling out hints to the lucky girl who got to choose. "Pick Number One," they hollered. "Number One." It wasn't all that late but Amanda was restless and distracted and cranky.

She stood next to Bill and tried to enter into the evening but she couldn't. "Are you ready to leave?" she asked.

"It's early," Bill said.

"I know, but . . ." She slipped her arm through his.

"Okay," he said. "At the end of this skit."

The contestant had chosen Bachelor Number Two and was squealing in delight. Bachelor Number Two, a well-known Hungarian minimalist, was hugging his date and slyly pulling up her stewardess outfit. Bill and Amanda made their way out of the crowded room and headed back to his apartment.

They made love wordlessly and there was a certain muscle in it, a certain antagonism, that had them rolling over and over, straining against each other. Amanda watched Bill's face contorted above her—I'm gonna huff and puff and blow your house down—and forgot for a moment whose face it was.

She lay awake long after he had started snoring and listened to a party going on upstairs. She lay awake and she listened to the loud, intimate laughter and to Bill's snoring and there was Nancy's one week and there was everything else and nothing was hers tonight.

Bill woke Amanda the next morning by rubbing coffee with his forefinger across her lips. He had already showered and was almost finished dressing, but he knew better than to try to talk to her so early. "I've got to go," he said. "There's an extra set of keys in the kitchen. Be sure to double-lock the door."

Amanda put her hand on his stomach and let it slide down to his belt buckle where it stayed for a minute. "Bill?"

"Yeah?"

"What do you think people owe each other?"

"What, now you want me to pay you for this?" He laughed. And then he looked down and stroked her forehead gently. "What are you talking about?"

"Never mind."

Bill stood up and knotted his tie. He stopped for a minute in the doorway and looked back at Amanda. "If it makes any difference," he said, "you're still my favorite partner in crime." And then he left for work.

Amanda got out of bed finally and put on one of Bill's crisp white Brooks Brothers shirts and went into the kitchen for some more coffee. She sat on the counter top and drank it while she stared at the multitude of scraps pinned to his bulletin board—phone numbers without names, invitations, an overdraft notice from the bank, a black-and-white photograph of Bill and an Amazonian model in the back room of a discotheque. When she had finished all of the coffee, she put on her pants and left, without unplugging the pot, without her own shirt, without double-locking the door.

Downstairs, Sam could hear his parents arguing about what television show to watch.

"It's a repeat, Fred," Mrs. Chapman said. "You've seen it already."

"I don't care," Mr. Chapman answered stubbornly. "I don't remember how it ends."

"But Fred, there's a game on . . ."

Sam got up and shut the door and then he paced restlessly about his small room, tapping with annoyance at the too familiar objects on the wall—the high school diploma and a copy of the first article he had published and a picture of him and Cathy at one of his sisters' weddings—he knocked angrily at them all, leaving the frames chaotically askew. Finally, he saw the softball lying on his pine Formica desk and he grabbed it and lay down on the single bed, tossing it up into the air and into his old glove, over and over and over again. He missed her too. Sam threw the ball too hard and it hit the ceiling. Then he lay completely still, hoping no one would come to see what the commotion was. No one did.

He began his game of catch again, methodical, repetitive, pointless. Some time later he heard his mother plod heavily up the stairs, grumbling to herself. "Technical foul my eye. That was no technical foul. I know my way around a court better than any frigging ref and that was no technical foul." The Cavaliers must have lost again.

It was close to three in the morning before Sam finally drifted into a skittish sleep, his glove beside him on the pillow. When the alarm went off a few hours later, he slammed his hand immediately down on the button and jumped briskly out of bed. He took a quick shower and went straight to work, filled with a cold sparky clarity that had him flying through his notes with a heightened determination and impatience. He took a break at lunch and called Cathy.

"I can't go to that dance after all," he said. "I've got to go to New York this weekend."

"What for?" Her voice was sharp with suspicion.

Sam held the receiver a couple of inches from his mouth. "Something to do with Mark's loft," he said quickly. "Something to do with the last article I did for *Backlog*."

"What?"

Sam's voice softened as if he were speaking to a child. "It's a quick flight, Cathy. I'll be back on Monday morning."

There was not much else Cathy could say. She said good-bye as disapprovingly as possible and she comforted herself with the thought that the odds were in her favor this time.

Sam relaxed a little as he finished up the article he was working on. It was easy now, easier than it had been for a long time. He had an insomniac's distorted energy, contorted reason, he had someplace to go. He took a deep breath. He knew now that he had to turn around, that like Orpheus, he had to have one last look, one last glance. Just to be sure.

And somewhere, deep inside, there was a little boy's voice desperately pleading: Tempt me. Lure me. Show me your very best. Show me something I can't refuse. Make me change my mind. Please.

"Do you want to come over for lunch?" Amanda asked Sally. "I thought I'd call Mom and see if she could make it. Maybe we could find out what's going on."

"Don't you have to go to work today?"

"I don't feel like it," Amanda said. "Nancy will understand."

"Are you sure?"

"Sure. How about one o'clock?"

"Fine. Amanda?"

"Yes?"

"Would you mind doing just a salad? I'm on a serious diet."

Mrs. Easton agreed, after much persuasion, to venture downtown and have lunch with her daughters. Amanda got dressed hurriedly and set out to the Korean market for fruits and vegetables and Perrier. She made a large salad and then she ran her fingers quickly through her apartment, throwing odd, inconsequential articles into the closet. There was always something she didn't want her family to see.

Sally arrived early with Maggie and a dozen toys spilling out of her oversized bag and sat down in her usual winded flurry.

"Well, have you told him yet?" Amanda asked.

"Told who what?"

"Have you told Frank you're leaving him?"

"Oh that." Sally switched Maggie's doll for a newer, dryer one. "I've changed my mind."

Amanda was more irritated by this than either of them would have expected. "It's because of the heart, isn't it?" she said sharply. "One stupid present and you change your entire mind."

Sally spoke calmly. "He's not some evil tyrant, you know. In a lot of ways, he's a very good husband. He doesn't drink, he doesn't mess around, he's dependable. It could be worse."

"It could be worse is not a reason to stay in a marriage. I just don't understand you," Amanda said with edgy frustration.

"No, I don't suppose you do. But who are you to be so judgmental?"

"I'm not judgmental."

"Yes you are. In your own way, you're just as judgmental as Frank."

"Look, Sally, you're the one who told me you were unhappy."

Sally looked at her sister and sighed. "Maybe I'm not as good at being alone as you are, Amanda."

Amanda did not answer this but only looked down at her watch impatiently. "Christ," she said. "It's almost one-thirty. I wonder what happened to her." She dialed her mother's number anxiously.

"Mom?"

"Yes, dear?"

"Where are you?"

"Why, I'm home."

"I can see that. But you're supposed to be here."

"Yes, dear. I suppose I've changed my mind. I really have so much to do here. Are you having a pleasant chat with your sister?"

"Lovely. Mom?"

"Yes?"

"Is Dad there?"

"Not at the moment, dear."

"What does that mean?"

"Well, he went back to Connecticut. To pick up a few of his things."

Sally, who had been holding her head next to Amanda's, grabbed the phone out of her hands.

"Is he drinking?" she almost yelled.

"Hello, Sally."

"Hello, Mom. Is he drinking?"

"Well, it's been a very difficult time for him, dear."

"I don't believe it. He's drinking and you're going to take him back. I give up."

"I have to run," Mrs. Easton said. "I thought I'd go to Saks and pick up some new sheets. Have a nice lunch."

Sally hung up the phone and looked at Amanda. "Don't say anything," she said. "I don't even want to think about it." And she gave Maggie a bottle of apple juice which she guzzled with her eyes closed in blissful satisfaction while Amanda served the salad.

"Did I tell you I ran into Nancy the other day?" Sally asked after a few minutes of distracted silence.

"No."

"She looks great. She's hardly even showing. So what's this about a partnership?"

"She told you about that?"

"I don't think she considers it a state secret. It sounds like a fantastic idea. Why don't you want to do it?"

"I didn't say I didn't want to do it."

"But?"

"But I'm just not sure I want to be that tied down."

"The queen of commitment," Sally muttered. "You have a million other opportunities that I don't know about?"

Amanda stood up to clear the table. "It's been a delightful lunch," she said. "Let's do it again real soon."

Jack answered the door holding a large glass of milk. "Amanda," he said, smiling widely. "Come in."

Nancy stuck her head out of Jack's study at the far end of the loft and smiled with surprise at seeing Amanda. "He's been following me around with that stuff since I got up," she said, motioning with horror at the milk. "It's enough to give anyone morning sickness. Come on in here where it's safe."

Amanda walked back and Nancy closed the door behind her. The small room was a kaleidoscopic whirlwind of supermarket cartons and books on the floor and papers seemingly in mid-air. The walls were a gray and white checkerboard where pictures had been removed and even the ceiling seemed turbulent.

"What on earth are you doing?" Amanda asked.

"Relocating Jack."

"Why?"

"Don't you think this would make a perfect little nursery?"

Amanda looked doubtfully at the somber lawyer's study. "Aren't you a bit early with this sort of thing?"

"Not at all. Besides, I want to get Jack used to the idea. Really, though, what do you think? A little wallpaper, a new light . . . Use your imagination . . . Think mobiles."

Amanda sat down carefully on one of the overstuffed corrugated boxes. "Sure. It'll be fine."

Nancy frowned and sat down on the floor opposite her. "Look, Amanda, before you say anything, I'm sorry about the other day."

"I'm sorry too."

"I shouldn't have said some of that stuff."

"Let's just forget it."

"Okay."

They sat there awkwardly for a couple of minutes, playing with the edges of cartons, ragged papers, strands of hair . . . Amanda wanted to reach over and wipe away the faint line of dust that ran down Nancy's cheek like a streak of gray tears. But she looked away instead.

"Let's try this again," Nancy said. "How would you like to be the official, legal, financial, moral and aesthetic partner in Legacies?"

Amanda laughed. "Well, if you put it like that . . ."

"I'll put it anyway you want it. Seriously, Amanda, it's not as if I wanted to chain you to the front door. But I really do need someone to share the responsibilities with, and the profits, I might add. If you want, we could give it a trial run."

"A trial run?"

"Sure. How about it?"

Amanda looked over at Nancy. "Okay."

Nancy gave a short, surprised laugh. "Okay? Just like that? Okay?"

"Okay." Amanda was beginning to laugh a little herself, for she was almost as surprised as Nancy.

"Okay," Nancy said and she went over to hug Amanda. But when she put her arms around her, the overloaded box tore open and Amanda landed flat out amid a lake of books. Jack knocked worriedly when he heard the crash and the hysterical laughter that followed. "Are you two okay in there?"

Nancy went and opened the door and, seeing that he was empty-handed, she kissed him lightly. "You've laid down your weapons?"

Amanda helped Nancy pack things up for an hour or two, laughing and sneezing from the dust, while Jack stood by and watched, groaning loudly. Before she left, she turned to Nancy solemnly. "One more thing," she said.

"Yes?" Nancy looked nervous.

"You really should drink your milk. It's important."

Sam stood outside the People Express terminal looking for the bus that would take him into the city when a young man grabbed his bag and started walking quickly away. "Hey, what are you doing?" Sam yelled. The man turned around impatiently and said, "C'mon, man, hurry up." Sam followed—he had no choice—until they got to a limousine a block away. "It's like this, man," the guy said as he threw Sam's bag into the back seat. "I had to make the trip out here, right? Well now I gotta go back empty. So this is the deal—I'll drive you in for the same it would cost you to take a cab. But if those hacks see me doing it they get all bent out of shape." He got in and started the engine.

So Sam rode into the city in the back of the limousine, watching all the time to be sure he wasn't being abducted and watching too the skyline, gray on gray in the late afternoon, growing larger and larger until they were inside of it and there was no skyline left. He was about to give the driver the address of Mark's loft when he changed his mind and decided to go straight to Legacies instead.

He paid the man and got out and stared at the "Sale" signs in the windows, recognizing with an uncomfortable lurch that it was Amanda's handwriting. He wanted, for just an instant, to yell for the limousine to come back. He couldn't remember deciding to come, he couldn't remember why.

Inside Legacies, Amanda was interviewing an odd assortment of men and women for a newly created part-time sales job. The applicants stood about in small clusters and lines—some dressed in low-heeled pumps and subtle stockings with freshly washed hair, and some looking as if the needles were still in their arms. It was Amanda's first real task as trial-run, full-time partner and there was a distinct tone of authority in her voice that sounded alien and pleasant in her ears. Nancy stood in the background and did not interfere.

At first, Amanda did not notice him, there were so many strange faces lurking about. And then it was as if she and Nancy both saw him at once. It stopped and it faded and they lost their footing for a moment and so did Sam. Amanda felt her face flush with embarrassment and she stood completely still, silent, waiting for the right words, the right attitude, to come to her.

Nancy broke through first. "Well I'll be damned," she exclaimed. "You're back." And she went up and gave Sam a big hug.

"Just for the weekend," Sam said, looking over her shoulder and smiling nervously at Amanda.

The job applicants were beginning to mumble and grumble, having lost interest in this little reunion scene, and Nancy looked about the confusion. Amanda ignored it all for one more minute and she went up to Sam and kissed him lightly on the cheek. "Hi."

"Hi."

They stood there for a minute not knowing what to do next.

"Can we go someplace and have a drink?" Sam asked.

Amanda looked about her at their disgruntled audience.

"Go ahead," Nancy said. "I'll take care of the rest of the interviews."

"No," Amanda said. She turned to Sam. "Can you wait a few minutes? I've got to finish up here."

"Sure," he said and he stepped back into the corner and watched her.

What was left of the sun bounced off of the ice and hit their eyes like a handful of nails—there was nothing warm about it. It was the same ice that had been freezing and melting and refreezing for weeks and the streets were a patchwork of filthy, treacherous slabs. Sam and Amanda walked in short hobbling steps toward the Homestyle Italian Cooking sign over one of Sam's favorite restaurants.

They settled in at a large corner table in the back, not quite next to each other, not quite opposite each other, and they embarked on an endless riff of nervous and polite chatter—how is your family and they're fine and how is your family and they're fine and how is your sister, fine, fine, fine—a verbal fumbling that they could not seem to stop. Amanda waited for Sam as if she were waiting for a salesman to stop his friendly banter and get to the pitch. But he could not seem to get there. Perhaps later, she thought, when we are alone in the dark, when my head is lying still against his chest . . .

Other people came and ate their dinners and Sam and Amanda drank a bottle of wine, noticing only that the table next to theirs was now empty, now full, now empty again. There was only this fumbling, tumbling, this low-level chatter of theirs . . . Perhaps later . . . A large calico cat played at Amanda's feet and it jumped up gratefully and snuggled in her arms when she motioned to it. Sam watched as she stroked it intently, dust rising from its coat, and he shuddered. He had always been terrified of cats. If only they could wipe it all away, he thought, wipe it all away . . .

He looked up at the register and watched as two middle-aged men paid their check and walked out holding hands.

"You know what Patrick wanted me to do before I left?" he asked.

"What?"

"A piece on a drag beauty contest."

Somehow it sounded as if this were Amanda's fault. "It might have been fun," she said petulantly.

Sam looked at her. If only they could wipe it all away . . . "Maybe," he said.

They were on opposite sides now, pushing and shoving, jockeying for position, arguing invisible points, backing up into indefensible positions. They were taking the longest possible route.

"There are other jobs, you know," Amanda said.

"I know. I just couldn't seem to land one."

"Did you think they were going to hand you the Pulitzer the minute you got inside the city limits?"

Sam did not answer.

At some point, they had ordered dinner and now it came and they stabbed at it and twirled it and finally pushed it away. It had nothing to do with anything. Sam embarked on a detailed description of the apartment he was considering in Allensville, which was of course twice the size and half the rent of anything he could hope to find in New York.

"But don't you miss the city?" Amanda asked suddenly. Perhaps later, perhaps now . . .

Sam was silent for a minute. "Sure I do. But I just wasn't getting anyplace here."

Amanda looked down, her cheeks as red as if she had been slapped in rebuke. Sam watched her for a moment. "Look, Amanda," he said and his voice was low and tired, exasperated now. "I need some security."

She looked up at him. "But . . ." They both leaned forward hopefully but it was a dense bramble of confusion and she did not finish her sentence. Sam sat back into the silence.

By the time they left the restaurant, it had turned into a hard-edged frigid night and they stood on the street corner shivering, suspended, not knowing where to go. Sam reached over abruptly and kissed Amanda good night. Both of their mouths were slightly open and his lips felt sad on hers.

She spent the night skidding off of sleep's surface and in the morning she was gaunt and green and her eyes were puffy orbs etched in black and she thought, He does not want me.

And she thought, He does not want me, while she swallowed three aspirin and made herself a pot of coffee. The pain had no edges, no shape, it just filled her all up—He does not want me—leaving her shell-shocked and dull. She sat motionless, lost in it. And yet, she gradually sensed something begin to cut into it, to pierce it, chase it away with a clean sharp blade, leaving a red gash through the fog. Anger.

Amanda was standing over the kitchen sink watching the black coffee she was pouring down the drain muddy the white porcelain when the doorbell rang. She looked suspiciously at the door for a minute, and yet poking its head through the wariness was the tiniest seed of hope.

"Who is it?" she asked, straightening her hair.

A voice, clean and young and not Sam's, answered with well-rehearsed optimism. "Hello, my name is Jaimie and I'd like to talk to you about the Horsemen and the Apocalypse." Amanda could feel him eagerly leaning forward.

There was a moment of absolute silence and then the harshly exaggerated loudness of Amanda putting the chain lock in place.

"Go fuck yourself," she said.

As she walked back into the kitchen, she could hear him ringing the neighbor's bell. "Hello, my name is Jaimie . . ."

The gash was deepening, widening, and she looked around for something to destroy. She took what was left of the coffee and threw it against the newly white wall, watching as the Plexiglas pot came apart in large triangular chunks and the coffee grounds dribbled slowly toward the floor. Then she went into the living room and picked up the phone.

"Thirty years old and you go home to your fucking mother," she yelled.

"Amanda?"

"What the hell are you doing here anyway?"

Sam let out a loud sigh, as if he had been holding his breath for an eternity. Here we are, he thought, we are finally here.

"I'm waiting for an answer. Why did you come back? Obviously not to talk to me. Not to sleep with me. Why?"

"I had to see you."

"Why?"

"Because . . ."

"I'll tell you why," Amanda interrupted. "You came back just to have a lousy time. Then you could go back all smug and sure of yourself and . . ."

"That's ridiculous. I told you, I came to see you."

"Oh, so that's what last night was? You seeing me?"

"Hold on. Last night was not completely my fault. You hardly said a word."

"Well I'm saying something now."

"After eight months." His voice was dry and bitter and it made Amanda pause.

"What the hell do you want from me?" she asked.

"I don't know," Sam said. "What do you want from me?"

"I don't know," Amanda answered impatiently, fearful that she was losing her point. "But I'll tell you something, you're not the only one who needs some security."

"I know that."

There was a long pause and the next time Amanda spoke it was in a low, low voice. "You lied to me, Sam."

"I never lied to you about anything."

"Yes you did."

"About what?"

There was a suspended silence and she could not find it, could not find the words, the lie, could not find anything, and so she quietly put her finger down on the button. Sam sat there for a few minutes, waiting for an answer, before he realized that she had cut them off.

She savored her anger, holding on to it with both hands, for it left no room for remorse, no space for a dangerous nostalgia. As it began to subside, she struggled to pull it back, summoning images of only their blackest moments, their dimmest mornings. But the most she could come up with was a general sense of distaste.

Amanda sat in the lobby of the Chelsea Hotel, waiting to meet with an English hat designer. He was already twenty minutes late and she sat with her sunglasses on, watching the afternoon parade of dusty old bohos and sharp-haired, knobby-kneed punks. When he finally came down from his room, it was obvious he had just woken up. He was a little man with round glassy eyes and the beginnings of a paunch and he was wearing a sleeveless fishnet top and black leather pants and velvet slippers with gold crests. "Darling," he said, "so sorry." He spread his portfolio across a wobbly coffee table. "Shall we have a look-see?" Amanda noticed that the crest on his left slipper was safety-pinned on.

She flipped through the photographs feeling empty and efficient. She knew in a minute that his creations were not right for Legacies. "I had hoped to see some of the hats in person," she said.

"Not possible, darling," the designer said. "They're all safe at home in London. Well, there are a few I loaned out the other night. Maybe you saw them . . ."

Amanda thanked him for his time and left the hotel. She stood for a minute on the noisy street, not knowing where to go, what to do. Sally lived three blocks away and despite the fact that she had never once just dropped in on her sister, Amanda decided to walk over there. There was always the chance that she'd have some Valiums.

Frank answered the door and they offered up shells of smiles to each other, like old foes who had laid down their arms but not forgotten the battles. "Come in," he said, and Amanda followed him into the living room, carefully stepping over the maze of toys and exercise equipment. Sally sat on the couch in a bright pink jogging suit and chatted obliviously on the phone while Maggie played at her feet, trying to eat her shoelaces. She nodded hello to Amanda and continued talking.

"How about some coffee?" Frank asked.

"Don't you have anything stronger?"

Frank poured her a drink disdainfully, ever on guard against one of these sisters blossoming into the alcoholic that all of the statistics warned against. Though of course, if it had to be one of them, it might as well be Amanda.

When Sally finally got off the phone she kissed Amanda hello and regarded her curiously for a moment. "Is everything okay?" she asked.

Amanda's throat caught unexpectedly, and she was just about to start talking when she saw that Frank had sat down opposite them, as stern as the Lincoln Memorial, and he made no sign of leaving. "Everything's fine," she said. "Just fine."

"Are you sure?"

"Sure."

The three of them proceeded to discuss aerobics versus Nautilus and Frank dragged out books to prove his point that you had to do both. Sally was on the floor demonstrating an upper-abdominal tuck when Amanda reached suddenly for her coat. "I really have to get going," she said, standing up. "Oh, by the way, do you have any Valiums?"

Sally, who usually stockpiled them, had recently increased her dosage by quite a bit and she had explained the missing pills to Frank by saying she had given them to Amanda. "I don't know," she said nervously now. "I'll go check." While she was gone, Frank turned to Amanda accusingly. "Be careful with those things," he warned.

Sally came back empty-handed. "Sorry," she said.

It was early evening when Amanda finally got home and she went straight to the bathroom and drew herself a scalding hot bath. She lowered herself into it inch by inch and then she lay there for hours, drinking brandy and smoking soggy cigarettes, only moving to burn an occasional hole through the bubbles.

When she got into bed that night, she was worn empty and hollow, and she fell into a deep comatose sleep, just barely interrupted every now and then by the sound of her own voice saying, "I'm not in right now, but if you leave your name and number, someone will get back to you . . ." and the sound of the crashing hang-ups, the furious dial tones.

He had never lied to her, never. Not once. He had never lied to her. It was she who had lied to him, with her silences and her evasions and her emotional disappearing act, she had never told him the truth, not once.

Sam slam-banged about the loft, picking up magazines and throwing them down, kicking at his duffel bag, rapping his fist against the window—she could not answer, she had cut him off, she never answered—until Mark, who was still trying to sleep, kindly asked him to leave.

He walked about aimlessly, trancelike, hardly aware of the traffic or the streets—crumbling, his plans were crumbling, he must have had plans, to wipe it all away—until, desperate for any sense of order, he headed for *Backlog*'s offices.

Patrick barely looked up when he walked in. "Sam," he said casually. "Good to see you. You looking for something to do?"

It was as if he had never left.

"Not really."

Patrick laughed indulgently. "I don't mean in general. I mean right now. I've got an emergency situation on my hands."

"What's the problem?"

"Peter was supposed to interview this Canadian director up at the Plaza and he didn't show up."

"The director?"

"No, Peter. Anyway, the director is fuming. I've got to get someone there pronto."

"Sure," Sam said. "Why not?"

Sam sat in a delicate gilt-edged velvet chair in the director's suite drinking pink champagne and watching roughly shot videos of the director's wife. They said little to each other, they just sat watching and drinking and every now and then, the director said, "Mmmmmm," as if there were some hidden meaning in the arch of his wife's foot. Sam excused himself and went to the phone. "I'm not in right now . . ."

"More champagne?" the director asked politely.

"Absolutely."

Sam never did get around to interviewing the man. After the first bottle was gone, he had called down for more and by then it was too late, all Sam could do was watch the videos in an appreciative silence. Every now and then, he went back to the phone. ". . . but if you leave your name and number . . ."

Finally, the director stood up and stretched. "Let's face it," he said. "Sex is the oddest darnn thing in the world." Sam looked up at him through skewered eyes and nodded gravely. And then he tried again. ". . . someone will get back to you . . ."

"I've got to go," he said resolutely.

He made his way through the hushed and stately lobby and down the majestic steps. The doorman made no sign of helping him find a cab and so Sam stood in front of the barren stone fountain, waving his arms desperately at every passing car.

He knocked until his knuckles were red and white and swollen. "Let me in, goddammit," he yelled at the thick steel door. "Let me in." Amanda came to the door just as her neighbor had opened his and was stepping out into the poorly lit hallway in his rumpled pajamas. "Do you want me to call the police?" he asked.

Amanda looked through her heavy dull eyes at the neighbor and then at Sam. "No," she said finally. "It's okay. I know him." The neighbor went reluctantly inside.

"Come in," she said wearily to Sam.

She did not turn the lights on and it took them a few minutes to adjust to the darkness softened only by the street lights seeping in. Sam paced up and down the length of the living room and Amanda sat on the couch with her legs tucked tightly beneath her, smoking a cigarette.

He stopped suddenly and leaned up against the wall facing her. "Why didn't you ask me to stay?" he demanded.

She filed the ashes at the end of her cigarette into a sharp glowing red cone. "Would it have made any difference?"

He shifted his weight from one foot to the other, almost losing his balance in the act. "Maybe," he said. "Maybe it would have. It would have helped."

"Helped what?"

"Just helped, that's all." He ran his hands through his hair, pushing his straight blond bangs off of his forehead again and again. "Did you want me to stay?"

She tried to look at him but her eyes slid off of his. "Yes," she said quietly. "I guess I did."

He started pacing again and she lit another cigarette from the end of the first one. "What did I ever lie to you about?" he asked.

"Never mind."

He stopped and laughed a little at this and she laughed a little too and then he came and sat next to her on the couch. His elbows rested on his knees and he held his head in both hands and she kept very still and they just sat like that for a while.

"Are you leaving again?" she asked finally.

"I don't know."

Amanda put out her cigarette. "That's really helpful. Why don't you know?"

He turned his head just slightly around toward her. "Maybe that depends on you."

"It can't all depend on me."

"No, I guess not."

They were speaking quietly now, as if they feared they might be overheard, and they were no longer on opposite sides, but somehow parallel to each other, looking out, trying to find it . . .

"We're going in circles, Sam."

He smiled helplessly at her. "Yes, I've noticed that."

She went to light another cigarette and he reached over with both hands and took it away from her and they froze, the palms of their hands against each other, their eyes locked. Slowly, she leaned back, and he followed and his face was next to hers . . . perhaps later, perhaps now . . . and their lips touched and bounced off of each other and touched again and stayed . . . wipe it all away . . . and there was nothing else left, there was only this, only this . . . and someplace deep inside the night, he thought he heard her say, I love you, and someplace she thought she heard him say, I love you, and perhaps it was better this way, dim, hazy, faraway, its edges blurred and malleable—for they could always claim amnesia in the morning.